"You think I'm a child, don't you?"

Amy's question was challenging.

"Sure," Mike replied. "Children cry at birthday parties when they're overexcited. And then they respond to being kissed better, cuddled and humored."

"You've humored me all you're going to," Amy said. "You can go and look after somebody else now!" It sounded ungracious, and that was how she felt. She didn't want Mike to get the wrong ideas about the effect his kisses had on her....

Amy didn't say good-night. She didn't even know when he'd gone. With the lights switched off, she looked out into the lovely starlit night.

Bangalo Island, she thought, a tropical paradise where people come to make a dream come true, just for a while. Where Amy Martin came when she woke and found her dream had vanished....

DOROTHY CORK
is also the author of these
Harlequin Romances

Barefoot Bride

by

DOROTHY CORK

Harlequin Books

TORONTO • LONDON • LOS ANGELES • AMSTERDAM
SYDNEY • HAMBURG • PARIS • STOCKHOLM • ATHENS • TOKYO

Original hardcover edition published in 1980
by Mills & Boon Limited

ISBN 0-373-02390-1

Harlequin edition published March 1981

Printed in U.S.A.

CHAPTER ONE

AMY MARTIN was scarcely conscious of the moist tropical wind that tossed her black hair across her eyes and flung her skirt against her bare legs as she stepped down from the plane into the afternoon heat.

She walked quickly towards the small airport buildings, looking eagerly ahead for Clifford. She was positive he would somehow manage to be there, in spite of the hastiness of her arrangements—her telegram that she was coming up to Cairns, his phone call two nights ago that he was 'busy as hell'. Clifford now ran, and owned, the sugar cane farm that had belonged to her Uncle Ralph, and it was the crushing season, but all the same, he would be there to meet her, she was sure.

'If you can't get away, Clifford,' she had said over the telephone with Aunt Evelyn hovering near, listening, 'Mrs Deluca will come to Cairns and meet the plane if you ask her. And Clifford, Aunt Evelyn thinks I should stay down the road with them—the Delucas— not with you. She says now Uncle Ralph's gone I shouldn't stay at the farm alone with you.'

'I guess she's right,' Clifford said, rather surprisingly, after a brief silence. Amy hadn't agreed with her aunt. She was quite sure she and Clifford could behave themselves even if they were alone—and about to plan the exact date of their wedding. But Aunt Evelyn had said, 'It's not fair to put that kind of strain on a man, and I certainly don't relish the idea of having my one and only niece pregnant before she's married. If you must rush off to Queensland now, Amy, instead of

5

seeing the year out in Sydney as I thought we'd all agreed was the sensible thing to do, then you're to stay with the Delucas. Do you understand?'

Amy had said she understood, but privately she determined to do as she pleased. After all, she had left school, she was nearly twenty, and she was engaged to be married, and no aunt, even if she was a headmistress, could push her around.

'But look here, Amy,' Clifford had continued, 'I don't know that the Delucas *can* put you up just now. The whole family's there, by the look of things. I'll check, of course, but it's a lot to ask of Mrs Deluca to drive all that way.'

'Well then, I'll stay at the farm with you,' said Amy. 'It'll be all right——'

'Not if your aunt doesn't like the idea,' Clifford said.

Amy had almost cried. It was so *stupid*. As if it *mattered* that Aunt Evelyn didn't like it——

'Whatever happens, I'm coming,' she had said. 'I'm not waiting till the end of the year, it's just too long. It was a silly idea in the first place. We're going to be married—I may be young, but I'm not likely ever to change my mind about you. And I—I want to see you *now.*'

'All right, I'll ring Mrs Deluca,' Clifford had said. 'And if the house is full up there, and if I can't get away myself—and I've told you I'm as busy as hell, Amy—then I'll arrange for you to stay in Cairns, say for a week. With the MacDonalds.'

'Who on earth are they?'

'Oh, nice people. They've only come to live in Cairns recently—they're retired from New Guinea. You'd better write down the address, unless you can wait another week or two.'

'Oh, Clifford, no! I've booked my seat on the plane —I'm all packed up.'

'Well then, have you got pen and paper handy?'

Amy had, and she wrote down the MacDonalds' address, and told him, 'But Clifford, I hope you can come, and that Mrs Deluca can have me. I don't want to stop in Cairns a whole week.'

'I'll do what I can,' Clifford had said. 'But if you will spring these things on me you can't expect them to work out without a hitch. I thought you were all set to stay where you were till at least Christmas.'

'I'm sorry, I—I thought you'd be pleased. *Aren't* you pleased, Clifford? I can't wait to see you again— it's been such an age. Not since February—not since you gave me my ring.'

'Yes, I know. But we talked about that, didn't we? And we decided not to rush it, so you could be sure.'

'I'm sure now, I have been all along,' Amy had said a little despairingly. 'I'm absolutely positive and I can't wait for a moment longer. Please Clifford, fix things up.'

'If I can,' Clifford had said.

And now Amy was hurrying across to the airport buildings in Cairns, praying that he would be there, or if not, that Mrs Deluca would be there. She was an Italian woman who lived with her husband on one of the cane farms down the road from Clifford, and Amy had known her since she was eight years old. That was when Amy's parents had been killed in a motor accident, and Ralph Martin had begun to share the responsibility for her with her mother's sister, Evelyn Dain. Holidays, except sometimes in summer, when the Wet made it unpleasant, Amy had always spent at the cane farm. The rest of the year she boarded at the school in Sydney where her aunt was headmistress.

Now she had almost reached the building with its airy grilled walls when someone caught her by the arm, and she looked round to find herself confronted by a fair-haired girl of about her own age—Karen Saunders, an old school friend. The two girls hugged each other and laughed with pleasure.

'Amy Martin! I thought it was you! I wish I'd seen you on the plane when I got on in Brisbane.'

'Karen!' Amy reciprocated. 'How lovely to see you! If we *had* spotted each other you could have sat next to me—there was an empty seat all ready waiting.'

'You've come all the way from Sydney?' Karen asked, as they continued on their way.

Amy nodded, her glance straying towards the crowd of people meeting the plane—the women in sleeveless dresses, the men in open-necked shirts and shorts. But there was not a sign of Clifford or Mrs Deluca, and she felt a surge of anxiety, though there was time yet for someone to arrive.

'There's my brother,' Karen exclaimed, and sped away in the direction of a tall broad-shouldered man on the far side of the building. Amy followed some distance behind. Coming up here in the plane for school holidays, she had seen Karen's brother often enough, but had never met him. He was years older than Karen, and he always stood out from everyone else, not only because he was so tall and always so well dressed, but for some other reason that she had never even tried to analyse. Charisma? she wondered now, looking at him obliquely. He wore white linen trousers, a dark blue casual shirt with a single button at the collarless neck, and he had the faintly laconic air of a very sophisticated man. For some reason, Amy felt nervous of meeting him, and she scanned the faces around her anxiously. Still no Clifford, and no plump comfortable Mrs Deluca. 'Blow!' she thought in dismay. It was beginning to look as though she might have to stay in Cairns, and she'd been so sure Clifford would move heaven and earth to see that she didn't. It wasn't fair!

Close to tears, she moved on, deliberately not joining Karen and her brother. Presently, the luggage from the plane would arrive on a trolley, and if no one turned up to meet her she would have to collect her bags and take the coach into Cairns, and then find her way by cab to the MacDonalds'. She just didn't believe it could happen. She'd never really doubted that Clifford would be there—that he would take charge of her two big suitcases, for one of which she had had to pay excess baggage, and both of which were crammed with clothes. Up-to-the-minute, sophisticated clothes, most of which she had made herself and which would put her right outside the just-left-school class and into the adult category—and give Clifford the surprise of his life. *And* have him convinced she was quite mature enough to have made up her mind whom she wanted to marry ...

A covert glance at the Saunders revealed that Karen's brother was looking in her direction. She blinked self-consciously, conscious of the tears on her dark lashes. Karen must have said something about her, and she had the distinct feeling that he was summing her up some way, and it made her uncomfortable. She turned away quickly to brush away her tears.

In another moment Karen had hurried and grabbed her by the arm. 'Come and meet my brother, Amy, while we watch for our luggage. Is anyone meeting you?'

'I hope so,' said Amy.

'Clifford?' Karen's grey eyes widened, and Amy nodded.

'Of course.'

Karen laughed and a moment later she was saying animatedly 'Mike, this is Amy Martin. Her uncle had a cane farm up here—and we were in the same class at school.'

Amy said 'Hello,' and gave him a restrained smile. She met his eyes, and discovered they were grey and lazy looking under thick peaked eyebrows that were part of the reason for his slightly weary air. He had light brown hair, thick and wavy on top but cut short enough to be well clear of his collar—if he'd been wearing one. It was a very stylish, very masculine cut that somehow added enormously to his general aura of sophistication and superiority. Of course, Karen's family would be sophisticated people. They ran a hotel resort on one of the tropical islands out towards the Great Barrier Reef. They wouldn't be exactly the kind of people Uncle Ralph—or Clifford either, for that matter—would mix with.

Mike had greeted her and he too smiled briefly and she thought, a little startled, 'What gorgeous teeth!' then glanced quickly away over his shoulder into the sunshine, to see if Clifford might have arrived in his car and be looking for her. He hadn't and he wasn't, but the luggage trolley was trundling into sight. Karen had moved away to talk to a middle-aged woman in a bright floral dress—an Italian, Amy guessed. There were lots of Italians up here in the tropics, growing bananas or pineapples, or sugar or tobacco, making a good life for themselves and their children.

She caught sight of her two suitcases, and with a murmured excuse moved over to the trolley.

'Let me,' said Mike Saunders from close behind her, and in a moment her two hefty bags were deposited on the ground beside her. 'Are you looking for a lift into town, or is someone meeting you, Amy?'

She glanced up. She was not a small girl, but he was over six feet, and for a moment his eyes explored hers penetratingly, before moving down to her wide un-painted mouth and then to her full-bosomed, trim-waisted figure in the yellow cotton dress.

Suddenly self-conscious, she dropped her lashes. 'I'm hoping to be met. By my fiancé, if he can make it.'

One eyebrow rose, and she knew she had surprised him. Yet he must be aware that she was Karen's age and quite old enough to be engaged, and if he had been observant, he would have seen she wore a ring. She raised her left hand deliberately to push back the dark hair from her cheek and allow him to see the pearl and diamond ring she wore and of which she was so proud. He saw it, and his eyes flicked over her again—assessingly. She hadn't liked being—looked at before, and she liked it even less now, but she pretended not to notice. It was a pity she was dressed so casually, she reflected—her dress so simple, her legs bare, and her hair messed up by the wind as well. She'd been practis-ing the mature look lately, for Clifford, who was ten years older than she was. Karen's brother was even older, she calculated. He looked to be well into his thirties and probably regarded herself and Karen as kids.

When he had done with looking her over he com-mented, 'Well, well, so you're an engaged woman. Is your boy-friend from Cairns?'

She flushed slightly. He could have said fiancé, and not boy-friend, she thought, annoyed.

'He lives up the coast,' she said rather shortly. 'Near Mossman. He's a cane farmer—Clifford North. I don't expect you know him.' She glanced at her watch as she spoke, as if to check when he'd be there.

'How long will you wait for him?' Mike Saunders asked.

'Oh, a little while,' she said vaguely. 'If he doesn't come I'll take the coach. He's pretty busy now, so I just might have to stay a night or two in Cairns.'

Karen rejoined them to say, 'My luggage, Mike—that red bag.' Obligingly he went to collect it for her and she asked Amy, 'Clifford not here yet?'

'No.' Amy sighed. 'I'm beginning to think he's not coming. As a matter of fact he's so busy just now it would have to be a miracle for him to turn up. And of course I was hoping for a miracle,' she added wryly. 'It's all my own fault, actually. I made a spur-of-the-moment decision and came racing up here.'

'I was surprised you didn't get married straight from school,' Karen remarked. 'We all expected it, you know. Then I ran into Maggie James and heard you hadn't. But it's still on?'

Amy's dark eyes widened. 'Of course! It's just that I was conned into waiting a year, and filling in with cooking and sewing classes.'

'By good old Dainie?'

'Yes, but by Clifford too. So he couldn't be accused of cradle-snatching, I suppose,' she added with a laugh. 'And now I've rebelled—I'm not waiting any longer.' She changed the subject quickly as Mike came back. 'What have you been doing this year, Karen?'

'I've been learning things too, in Brisbane. Typing and book-keeping,' said Karen, fingering the gold sleepers in her ears, obviously new. 'I'm going to start working at the hotel now—aren't I, Mike?'

'That's right. And working's the operative word.' He turned to Amy. 'Well? Are you still waiting?'

She shrugged. 'I guess not. I don't think Clifford's

going to make it today.' Nor Mrs Deluca either, she thought resignedly.

'What will you do?' Karen asked. 'See if you can pick up a ride to Mossman?'

Amy shook her head. 'Clifford has some friends in Cairns I can stay with.'

'Then we can give you a lift,' said Karen. 'Can't we, Mike?'

'Sure. Let's go, then.' Despite her protests, he took both of Amy's bags while Karen carried her own—a much smaller one, certainly—and the two girls followed him over to the car in the blindingly bright sunlight.

'Where in Cairns?' he asked Amy when they were all installed, she in the back seat, Karen beside him in the front, and they had started on the five and a half kilometre drive into town.

'Whitfield,' she said, and gave him the address. 'I hope it won't keep you late. Are you going across to Bangalo Island today?'

Karen half turned round in the front seat to answer her.

'We're spending a day or two in Cairns. Mike has a house in town right near the bay. He has some waitresses to interview, and I want to look up a few people before I start work. Couldn't you stay with us, Amy? There's plenty of room.'

'Look, Karen,' Mike put in firmly, 'don't try to rearrange other people's plans. Amy's boy-friend's fixed everything up for her, let it stand.'

Amy sat back in the seat. Her heart had leapt at Karen's invitation. She was desperately disappointed that Clifford hadn't come, that it seemed the Delucas couldn't have her, and she didn't look forward to staying with people she didn't know. She had always liked Karen, but obviously her brother wasn't eager to endure her company. He had knocked back Karen's proposal very smartly so that Amy hadn't been given the opportunity to accept or to refuse it. She began to think he must be one of those men who like to order things their own way—though perhaps most men were like that. Even Clifford, if she really thought about it.

She thrilled as she always did when they reached town. She adored Cairns with its tall coconut palms, its wide streets where tropical trees flowered and the footpaths were shaded by huge mango trees. The gardens were brilliant with flowers—hibiscus, frangipanis, gorgeous bougainvilleas—and green ferns and other exotic blooms clustered about the houses, most of them built up on stilts for coolness: 'Hi set', as they put it in the ads, a style Amy loved. Her uncle's house at the cane farm in Mossman—Clifford's house now, and soon to be hers—was red cedar and set high on stilts with a cool recreation area underneath.

Mike located the MacDonalds' house—a small brick home on a corner block, with an enclosed area underneath and a landscaped garden. He pulled up near the gate, got out of the car, opened Amy's door for her, then went to the trunk for her luggage.

'It's been lovely to meet up with you again,' said Karen. 'Let's know about the wedding, won't you? Send me an invitation!'

'Of course,' Amy agreed. 'But it will probably be in Sydney. Aunt Evelyn wants me to be married in the school chapel, and have the reception at the school too. I don't know what Clifford will think of the idea, because most of his friends live up here.'

'Still, it's your day,' Karen commented. 'You have it your way, Amy. Anyhow, keep me posted—care of Hotel Bangalo will find me. We'll probably see something of each other if we're both living up this way.'

'I hope so.' The two girls smiled at each other and clasped hands briefly. By the time Amy got out of the car, Mike was waiting for her and looking rather impatient, her two bags on the grass at his feet. He said nothing but picked them up and walked towards the house. She followed him, and it was on the tip of her tongue to apologise for keeping him waiting, but why should she? She'd only been saying goodbye to Karen. There was no need for him to be so cranky.

He said over his shoulder, 'By the look of the windows, nobody's at home.'

'It doesn't matter. I can wait in the garden. Clifford will have contacted them.'

He looked sceptical as they climbed the steps to the front door and rang the bell. Nobody came, and after a minute Mike remarked, 'So much for your boyfriend's arrangements. They don't appear to be working too well.'

'My *fiancé's* arrangements, you mean,' Amy said coldly. 'And of course they're working. You don't need to make a fuss. You can go on to wherever you're going and forget me. The MacDonalds will be back.' She turned her back on him and gritted her teeth. Nothing was going right today, and his attitude didn't help.

'I'll check with the neighbours before I leave you, all the same,' he said.

Amy shrugged. 'Go ahead. But I keep telling you—it will be all right.'

She watched him go back down the steps through the garden, then along to the house next door. 'They're just out shopping,' she told herself. Or possibly they'd gone out to the aerodrome to meet her and they'd missed each other. Of course! That must be it! She ran down the steps and dashed across the lawn to the low fence that divided the two gardens, ready to tell him the conclusion she'd reached, but he was already talking to the neighbour and she could hear the conversation clearly.

'What a good thing you thought to call in! I'd meant to be looking out for Miss Martin, and it slipped my mind. I'm afraid the MacDonalds had to leave for Townsville this morning. Their daughter's been expecting a baby and her husband rang at about ten to say she'd been taken to hospital prematurely. Irene had promised to look after the other two little ones, so she just had to go. She asked me to watch out and explain what had happened.'

'I see,' Mike said courteously—far more courteously than he had spoken to her, Amy thought a little resentfully. No doubt he was pleased to discover that her 'boy-friend's' arrangements had come to grief!

'Irene suggested I advise Miss Martin to go to a motel and ring her cousin from there this evening. So if you could tell her——'

'Certainly,' said Mike. 'Don't you worry, I'll look after Miss Martin.'

'Will you? I'm so glad the poor girl didn't come on her own—that she has friends.'

Amy, listening, was feeling rocked. Her cousin! How about her *fiancé*? And who on earth had decided that Clifford was her cousin? That stupid woman next door, no doubt—whom she couldn't see and didn't want to. So now what was she going to do? Oh, if only Mossman wasn't so far away! Perhaps she could hire a car—with a driver, it would have to be, because she didn't have a driving licence. She did have three thousand four hundred and forty-nine dollars though, the remains of the five thousand Uncle Ralph had left her. She could afford a taxi to take her the seventy-odd kilometres to Mossman, so why not?

Well, why not? Some sixth sense seemed to be warning her not to be impulsive a second time, not to rush it. To wait, think, to telephone Clifford first.

Mike by now was coming back. Damn him, she thought angrily, and rather unjustly because of course it wasn't his fault.

'I heard,' she said when he was near enough. 'I'll go to a motel, the Tradewinds. If you could drop me off there——'

He was looking at her thoughtfully, his grey eyes sardonic. 'You'll ring Clifford from there tonight, will you? Is he your cousin?'

'No, he's not,' she said shortly. She wasn't going to explain that possibly, because Clifford had worked for her uncle at the cane farm for quite a long time, some people might think he and she were cousins—that Ralph was his uncle as well as hers. She turned her back on Mike and went back for her luggage and he followed her, and wrested the bags from her. She gave in after a short struggle and discovered she was panting. She didn't know why, but somewhere deep inside she was beginning to be frightened. It was all getting a little nightmare-like.

Back at the car she told Karen what had happened and what she planned to do.

'You're not going to let Amy go to a motel, Mike!' Karen exclaimed incredulously as, having once more stowed away Amy's luggage, he got back into the car. 'She can come with us now—of course she can!'

Amy bit her lower lip because it was trembling. She wanted to protest, but all she could manage was a rather wavering, 'It's quite all right, Karen—I——'

'Oh, don't let's make a big thing of it,' snapped Mike. He put the car into gear and started off with a jerk. 'Karen's invited you to my home, so you might as well accept graciously. You've obviously been stranded.'

Amy sank back in the seat and closed her eyes. What a way to put it! She couldn't have felt less welcome. But there was nothing she could say now, and she only hoped that, when she rang Clifford tonight, he'd somehow manage to come and collect her tomorrow and the whole thing would be settled.

'How long have you been engaged, Amy?' Mike asked a couple of minutes later, and she brightened up at his tone. Maybe he was sorry for his brusqueness and was trying to make amends by showing a little human interest in her.

'Officially, since February,' she said, sitting forward and unconsciously fingering her engagement ring.

'And unofficially?' he asked dryly, and she discovered he was looking at her through the rear vision mirror.

'Since October last year, just before my uncle died. He was very ill in hospital and he wanted——'

The peaked eyebrows rose. 'Good God! A deathbed promise. Practically a guarantee of disaster if you hold each other to it.'

Amy flinched. 'It wasn't like that at all,' she exclaimed, her pulses quickening protestingly. 'I've always wanted to marry Clifford. Uncle Ralph just wanted to know it was all settled.' She paused, uncertain whether to say more or not, then decided she would, if only to take that knowing, sceptical look off Mike Saunders' much too sophisticated face. She shifted along the seat a little so he couldn't stare at her before she went on. 'As it happens, I've been in love with Clifford for years and years—practically ever since he came to work for my uncle when I was about fourteen.'

'She has, Mike,' Karen put in. 'Amy was *always* talking about Clifford North at school. Gosh, I can't remember a time when she wasn't. We all used to think it was terribly romantic, and it made her quite different from the rest of us. Of course you *were* different from the regular boarders, weren't you, Amy? You weren't cooped up in a dorm like us, giggling and gossiping about guys, and really knowing nothing about them. Miss Dain is Amy's aunt,' she explained to her brother, 'so Amy lived in her bungalow. I didn't really envy you that, Amy, I must admit.'

'I didn't mind it,' Amy said defensively. 'I got on well with Aunt Evelyn.'

'Hmm,' Mike murmured consideringly. 'I'd been wondering about that little air of yours, Amy. Having a headmistress for an aunt and an idyllic romance dating back to your early teens and still going strong certainly explains a lot.'

What did it explain? Amy had no idea how to take his remarks, but she had a distinct feeling he was making a dig at her, and she couldn't stop herself from asking aggressively, 'What do you mean? That I seem older than Karen?'

'Good lord, no! Definitely not.' He negotiated a corner and then continued, 'You're like—well, let's see, how can I put it? Like a little girl with her eyes fixed firmly on the cake—and the pretty birthday candles. I rather suspect you've been at it for so long it would take a major disaster to divert you by now.'

Amy listened, puzzled and uncomfortable. He was obviously making fun of her and she couldn't see why, and she didn't like it.

'I'm afraid I haven't the least idea what you're talking about,' she said, aware of the resentment and antagonism in her voice.

'I don't suppose you have,' he agreed. 'And that's precisely because you're so preoccupied with those candles.'

'Mike!' Karen broke in protestingly. 'What on earth are you going on about? You're acting like a rude pig, and I hate that. What's got into you?'

'Nothing, nothing ... What do you think, Amy? Do you share Karen's opinion and think me rude?'

Amy did, but as well she thought him hateful and deliberately hurtful. Only she wasn't going to give him the satisfaction of knowing it.

'I think you're trying to be clever,' she said. 'And I don't really care what you think about me.'

'Don't you?' he said mockingly.

'No, I don't,' she snapped, and knew that it was a lie. Stupidly, she did care, and she was hurt. He had somehow stirred an uneasiness in her, though she wasn't sure why, and she longed to tell him that she'd changed her mind, she wasn't going to stay in his house, not even for a night. She'd rather go to the motel. She moistened her lips, swallowed slightly and hesitated.

And then Karen said, 'Well, there you are, Mike. Amy's not going to take any notice of you, and I'm glad. You're beastly, and I wish you'd shut up and stop treating us like a couple of school kids. Anyhow, shouldn't we find a shop and buy something for dinner before we go home? Seeing you only flew over this afternoon I don't expect there's anything much to eat in the house.'

'We'll eat out,' he said, then asked ironically, 'Will that suit you, Amy?'

'Whatever you say,' shrugged Amy. 'You're the

host.' And think that over, she added inwardly, hoping it would somehow point up his deficiencies. She made a rapid decision that tonight—if they ate out, she'd soon show him she wasn't a little girl of any kind. She'd wear something sophisticated and she'd act to match it. She might, in fact, be just a little bored with Mike Saunders and let him know it . . .

His bungalow was old and beautiful, smothered in exotic tropical plants. Obviously, since he must live mostly on Bangalo Island, he must employ a gardener to keep the garden in such beautiful shape. Inside, Amy had a bedroom to herself—a big airy room with a ceiling fan and greenery at the wide windows. Mike went out in the car again, ten minutes or so after they had arrived, leaving the girls to do as they pleased. After they had hung up some of their clothes and changed, they went under the house to relax. It was cool there, and there was cane furniture and even a small refrigerator, stocked with cold drinks.

Sipping pineapple juice, Karen talked enthusiastically about working at the Hotel Bangalo.

'It would be beaut if you could come over there, Amy. Mike's lifted it right out of the slightly Spartan, which is the way it was in Father's time, so now it's a really top-rate swinging holiday resort—not so sophisticated it would frighten anyone off, but lots of fun. The food's super—he has a marvellous chef—and the entertainment's great. There's a fantastic little dance band. How about spending your honeymoon there? You could suggest it to Clifford.'

Amy didn't think so. She didn't fancy spending her honeymoon at a hotel run by Mike Saunders. Besides, it would probably be phenomenally expensive, and Clifford just wasn't phenomenally wealthy. He was very comfortably off, of course, because Uncle Ralph had left the cane farm to him, but anyhow, she didn't want to go to the Hotel Bangalo for her honeymoon.

'I don't know what Clifford plans,' she told Karen tactfully. 'And I don't actually know when we'll be married. I hope it will be soon, but we might have to wait till the Wet when Clifford can take more time off.'

'Well, you never know, he might go mad and decide to snatch you up and whisk you off to a tropical island right away,' said Karen with a grin. 'Now you're here he won't want to wait any longer, I'll bet. He's given you a fair chance to wriggle off the hook if you saw someone you liked better, and obviously you haven't . . . What's he like, your Clifford?'

Amy leaning back in her chair, turned her glass in her hand. 'Clifford? Well, he's—he's thinnish—very good-looking, with dark hair. About five foot ten——'

'Yes, but what's he like as a man?' Karen persisted. 'I mean, you've been mad about him so long——'

'Well, he's just—awfully nice, I suppose,' Amy said lamely after a moment. It was hard to say what Clifford was like as a man. He had always taken a lot of notice of her, always been kind—given her birthday presents, listened when she wanted to talk, helped her cook the meals sometimes——

'Awfully nice!' Karen exclaimed, laughing. 'Come on, Amy, there's more to it than that! Is he—well, passionate? Sexy?'

Amy blushed scarlet and stooped to put her glass on the floor and hide her burning cheeks.

'I'm not asking if you've slept with him,' Karen said after a moment. 'Knowing you, and knowing Ev Dain, I guess you haven't. But he's kissed you and all that sort of thing—you must know if he's passionate. But I suppose I shouldn't ask you such things—I'm being almost as rude as Mike. It's just that I used to wonder at school what it was like to—well to be in love, really in love. You always had such a virginal look and yet you had a boy-friend long before any of the rest of us. A serious one, I mean.' She tossed back her silky blonde hair and fingered her gold earrings. 'Do you want another drink?' She reached for the jug, filled up Amy's glass and then her own.

'Thanks,' said Amy. Karen was trying to cover up, but she sensed that something further was required of her, that she should say something more about Clifford, if only to show Karen she didn't think her rude. The fact was, she'd never really thought about whether or not Clifford was sexy. Women liked him, so she supposed he was.

'I—guess he's sexy,' she said awkwardly. 'I'm probably lucky he's waited for me instead of marrying somebody else. He's nearly thirty, you know.'

'Um, nice and mature. I like mature men,' Karen took a drink and ran her tongue along her upper lip. 'There are some fantastic guys on Bangalo Island. Mike's assistant, for one—Paul Richards. He looks after everything whenever Mike's away. I'll be in the office for a start, sort of behind the scenes, learning about the financial side of it all. But I'll be able to mix with the guests if I want to, not like the waitresses and housemaids and most of the rest of the staff. After all, I'm the boss's sister, and a shareholder in the company as well, so Mike can't push me around just any way he wants. Father fixed up years ago for me and Pauline to be shareholders when he made the business a company.'

Thankful that the conversation had taken a new direction, Amy asked, 'Is Pauline working there too? I didn't know her very well at school, she was too far ahead of us.'

'Four years,' Karen agreed. 'She was working at the hotel. Mike insists we have to know something about it as we're part of it. But she went and fell in love with an Italian guy who'd come to play guitar with the band. Mike didn't like it and he sacked Sandro, and Pauli cleared out and married him and now they've gone off to Italy. Mike's furious. He's convinced all Sandro wants is her money.'

He would think that, Amy caught herself reflecting. Aloud she asked, 'And what do you think? Pauline's frightfully pretty, after all.'

Karen grimaced. 'Yes, but—oh, I don't know—I don't think she should have rushed into marriage. Sandro's only twenty-one and he has nothing. His family are pretty upset about it too. They grow sugar a few miles out of town—his mother, and three brothers, two of them married. Sandro is the youngest of the family and a bit of a problem. They didn't want him to go to Bangalo, they wanted him on the farm. His mother was terribly cut up when he and Pauli got married at the register office without telling anyone. And that reminds me, I'm going to ring her. And if they ask me to dinner tonight I'll go. Mike probably won't be pleased, but they might have some news. We just don't know where they are at the moment.'

She went inside and Amy stayed where she was to finish her pineapple juice. She felt sorry for Pauline and didn't quite know what to make of the marriage. Probably if Mike hadn't sacked Sandro, she reflected, Pauline would have got over her infatuation. 'Thank goodness there's no chance of anyone marrying me for my money,' she thought. Her uncle had left her five thousand dollars, and that was all she'd ever had. He had left the farm to Clifford, which was only fair, because Clifford had been his right-hand man for years and knew how to run it. Amy herself was his only living relative, and she knew he had always had doubts about leaving the property to a female, fond of her though he was. She didn't know if he had made a will before he discovered how ill he was, but then he had left the farm to Clifford, and died happy, with Clifford's assurance that he and Amy would marry each other. So it had all worked out very satisfactorily.

Of course, if the cane farm had been left to her, then someone might have married her for her money—even though it was peanuts compared, say, with the Saunders' hotel business.

'*Really* peanuts,' she reflected with wry amusement. Uncle Ralph had certainly indulged her a little, but he had been able to do that mainly because all her schooling was taken care of by Aunt Evelyn.

She finished her drink, rinsed her glass, and went up the steps to the porch. There was smoke on the evening air, and she knew it was from cane that was being fired in preparation for harvesting next day. Probably up at Mossman Clifford too was busy burning off a field. She knew sufficient about cane farming to be aware that when the cane inspector from the mill directed a certain quantity of cane to be cut at a certain time, then it must be done. It wasn't left to the discretion of the individual cane farmers. Burning, harvesting and transport of the cut cane to the mills were carefully organised to a detailed timetable over the whole of the crushing season, which lasted from June to December. This meant that the mills worked at full capacity and that the cut cane didn't deteriorate through not being crushed as soon as possible. And it was the reason why Clifford hadn't been able to get away today.

Standing on the porch of Mike Saunders' house in

Cairns, Amy thought nostalgically of other years, when she'd been at her uncle's farm when the cane was being harvested. She remembered the excitement of watching the cane being fired to remove weeds and trash before the big mechanical harvesters came in the next day. Men stood by ready with wet bags in case the flames should jump the fire break, and then there would be the deafening roar as the cane was fired and the flames leaped forty feet into the air and raced across the cane field. The late afternoon sky was blackened as the burnt leaves and trash were carried upwards and upwards on the tremendous waves of heat.

With a feeling of restlessness she went inside to find Karen turning from the telephone, her grey eyes bright.

'The Fiorenzas have asked me to dinner,' she exclaimed. 'Such lovely warm Italian people! If only Pauli had fallen in love with Gianni, Mike would have accepted it, I'm positive. He's coming to pick me up in half an hour anyhow, so I must hurry. If Mike isn't in before I leave, tell him where I've gone, there's a dear.'

'Okay,' Amy agreed, and sending her a flashing smile, Karen raced off to get ready, leaving Amy to reflect without much joy that now she would have to dine alone with Mike Saunders. She couldn't see any way of getting out of it, and she didn't look forward to it one little bit.

When Karen had finished with the shower, she had her turn and she had just returned to her room when the doorbell rang, announcing Gianni's arrival. Karen, looking very pretty in apricot silk and long earrings made of fine gold chain, put her head around Amy's door to say goodbye before she hurried away. Amy felt a little disappointed not to be meeting Gianni. She had already instructed Karen to ask if the Fiorenzas knew Clifford by any chance, but she would have liked to ask

Gianni herself. She thought with a little thrill of excitement of the fun it would be, meeting Clifford's friends, forming part of a group of young married people. It wasn't very likely, actually, that the Fiorenzas would know Clifford. Their cane would go to the Hambledon Sugar Mills in Cairns, whereas Clifford was associated with the Mossman Mill, some seventy kilometres distant. Still, you never knew, and it would be a point of contact, a beginning. She could imagine herself teling Clifford, 'I met some awfully nice people who grow sugar. Let's drive down to Cairns one weekend and look them up. They'd love it—they're Italians, so warm and friendly.'

When Karen had gone, she continued with her dressing. She chose a black silky sleeveless dress with scalloping at the hemline and around the deep V neckline. A wide soft belt showed off her small waist and emphasised the curves of her hips and bosom. Red high-heeled sandals went on her feet, and she used a bright red lipstick that looked good against her lightly tanned skin and showed up the darkness of her eyes. She parted her black hair in the centre and sleeked it down to turn inwards just above her shoulders, using a little hair-spray to hold it in place. Perfume—a dab of Joy that Clifford had given her two Christmases ago and that she knew was madly expensive.

She looked, she decided, a good twenty-five.

She was in the sitting room looking through a magazine and pretending to herself that she wasn't feeling nervous when she heard the front door, and a moment later Mike looked into the room.

'Where's Karen?'

'She went out to dinner with some Italians,' Amy said casually, and saw his jaw tighten and his grey eyes narrow.

'I see. Well, you certainly look as if you're all dressed up and expecting to go out.'

The blood rushed to her cheeks and she stiffened, feeling herself bristle with hostility.

'I thought you said we'd eat out.'

'I did,' he agreed. 'Well, get yourself a drink while I shower. And pour me a Scotch while you're at it,' he concluded as he made for the door.

Amy looked after him helplessly. Aunt Evelyn didn't drink, and Uncle Ralph and Clifford had confined their drinking mainly to NQ Lager or Cairns Draught. There was a cocktail cabinet in the room and she found the Scotch and a glass that she hoped would be suitable, then went to the kitchen for ice and water. Now what did she do? she wondered, returning reluctantly to the 'bar'. Did she pour the Scotch? And how much ice and water did she add? And—was he going to drink it in his bedroom—or even in the bathroom? Should she go and ask him?

Definitely not, she decided. If he wanted it now, he could come and get it.

She inspected the other bottles, unscrewed a bottle of Bacardi and sniffed at it. It reminded her of some toffee she used to like, but she didn't think she'd better drink any of it. She'd have to pour out something for herself, she supposed, and she looked rather longingly at a bottle of orange juice. But she wasn't going to make much of an impression as a sophisticate if she chose that, so she forbore.

She was still fiddling about undecidedly when Mike came back into the room, his hair wet, his chest brown and bare above dark olive pants. His eyes were sharp as chips of ice as he came to join her and take over.

She said nothing as he splashed Scotch into a glass,

ignoring the water and the ice, which was beginning to melt.

'What's been holding you up?' he asked mockingly. 'Don't you know which is my bedroom?'

Of course she did, but swallowed nervously and retorted, 'You didn't say you wanted it in your room. I—I calculated if you wanted a drink before you showered, then you'd come and get it.'

'Did you? Then maybe it's just as well. You'd probably have drowned it, judging by the preparations you've been making. Haven't you had a drink yet? Or don't headmistresses' nieces imbibe?'

'Headmistresses' nieces are no different from other girls,' Amy retorted, stung because she wasn't making the impression she had planned. 'So I wish you'd stop harping on something that's not significant. I haven't had a drink because I was waiting for you.'

'What's it to be, then?' he said briskly.

'Sherry,' said Amy, mainly because she couldn't think of anything else. Then when he had poured it and she had taken a sip, she wished she'd settled for orange juice. It was so dry!

He didn't miss out on her reaction, though she did her best to hide it, but to her relief he left her alone again, taking his glass with him while he finished dressing. She sat down on the arm of one of the chairs and doggedly attacked her sherry again. She might, she decided with a rather bitter amusement, find she needed the assistance of a little alcohol, if she was going to have to spend the evening with that rather ghastly and intimidating man who seemed all set out to take her down a peg whenever possible.

Well, at least she had a legitimate reason for wanting to come home early. She had to ring Clifford.

CHAPTER TWO

'DID you telephone your fiancé?' he asked a few minutes later when he rejoined her, wearing, now, a terracotta-coloured silk shirt that looked both dressy and casual at the same time—very much Cairns, in fact—and gave his skin a warm and vital look.

'I'll wait till we come back,' Amy said. She swallowed the last of the sherry with an effort and managed not to make a face. 'I want to have plenty of time to talk.'

'Of course. Well, shall we go?'

She stood up at once and followed him from the room, and as he opened the front door for her he said, his voice very close to her ear, 'I forgot to tell you how ravishing you look. Though for my taste, your lipstick's a little too lush. If you're hungry, you're going to have a problem keeping it looking like that.'

'Am I?' she said indifferently, though inwardly she was thinking, 'Here we go again!' 'Well, it's not going to worry me particularly, and as a matter of fact,' she concluded, moving quickly ahead of him down the steps. 'I didn't give a thought as to what your taste might be when I made up.'

'Remiss of you,' he drawled. 'Seeing I'm taking you out to dinner.'

'Oh? I thought we were just—just eating out.'

He took her arm at the foot of the steps and she tried to wriggle away from him, but he tightened his grip. 'Did you now? Yet you're dressed very much like a girl who's being taken out to dinner. And that perfume you're wearing—special occasion stuff ... I hope you

30

won't mind if we walk instead of taking the car. We're only going a couple of blocks and I took note that your heels aren't extra high.'

'Walking suits me fine,' she said. 'But I wish you'd stop clutching my arm.'

'By all means.' He released her at once and they walked in silence. Amy tried to enjoy the pleasant warmth of the night, but found she was too conscious of the man at her side to do so. She felt horribly uncomfortable with him, aware as she was that for some reason he didn't seem to like her. She tried to think of something to say—something harmless, but something that wouldn't be a dead end remark. It would be tactless to ask about Pauline under the circumstances or to mention Karen's going to dinner with the Fiorenzas, and she didn't want to talk about herself and Clifford. Finally in desperation, she asked, 'Are you married, Mike?'

'No. What makes you ask? Personal interest—female inquisitiveness?'

Her cheeks flamed in the darkness. 'I just wondered, that's all.'

'Well, now you know. I'm not married and not planning to be in the near future ... Shall we go in here to eat?' He touched her arm and directed her to the entrance of a restaurant attached to one of the best motels in town. As she went inside with him, she gave herself a mental reminder that she had decided to act sophisticated, bored, but she didn't like her chances. Mike chose a table in an inner courtyard where the lights were low and the shadows of tall feathery bamboos lay against the sky.

They had ice cold vichyssoise followed by mud-crab and salad, and they drank white wine—Amy warily as she wasn't used to it and didn't want to make a fool of herself. She felt self-conscious about her lipstick, mainly because Mike seemed to look at her mouth so often, but she forced herself not to worry about it. She'd renew it at the end of the meal. She wasn't going to spoil her enjoyment of the delicious mud-crab by watching out for her make-up. She wished it was Clifford sitting opposite her. He had only ever taken her out to dinner once, and that had been early in the year in Sydney, when he had bought her ring. She hadn't in fact come to Queensland since she had left school because this year was supposed to be a testing time as well as a time for learning some practical skills. And she'd cut it short——

'More wine, Amy?' the handsome man across the table asked, and she started and covered her glass quickly with her hand. She was feeling just the faintest bit muzzy.

'No, thank you, I've had enough.'

'And I can't tempt you to have just a little bit more than enough?' he said mockingly, refilling his own glass.

'Headmistresses' nieces are never tempted to have more than enough,' Amy heard herself say smartly, and the very fact that she said such a thing was sure proof that she'd already drunk more than she should have.

Mike looked at her amusedly, his mouth curving upwards crookedly. 'Okay, that was certainly in my mind, but I wasn't going to say it. And by the way, if you want to restore the seductiveness to your mouth, go ahead, don't mind me. You've lost the lot, you know.'

'I thought you didn't like it,' she said perversely.

'And I thought you didn't care,' he mocked.

'I—I don't. But I'll wait till the end of the meal.' She reached out and played with her glass, and jumped nervously when he leaned forward and asked her in a low voice, 'Amy, just how keen are you on getting married?'

What a question! And the way he asked it—and the way he was looking at her. She could feel the racing of her heart as she answered flusteredly, 'I—I want to, of course. It's what I've always wanted most.'

He continued to look at her across the table, took cigarettes from his pants pocket, and asked her absently, 'Dessert?'

'No, thank you.'

'Cigarette?'

She shook her head, and he put the packet away again. Smoking—another thing headmistresses' nieces didn't do, she supposed he was thinking. So perhaps she should have accepted a cigarette, but it was too late now.

'It's all you want, then,' he said as though their conversation hadn't been broken. 'No ambitions, no career.'

'No.'

'Just—marriage. Straight from school to the bridal bed, via the odd lesson in cookery and stitchery. And your aunt, the admirable Miss Dain—we've met, you know—she approves?'

'Yes, of course. Why shouldn't she?' She was defensive.

'I'd have thought, being a career woman herself, she might have had ambitions for you, so why such unquestionable approval? Though I seem to recall that your uncle was all in favour too. Didn't you say your fiancé worked for him, by the way?'

'Yes.' Amy discovered she couldn't think straight, and she tried to remember exactly what she'd told Mike about Clifford—and remembered his comment, 'A deathbed promise'. She said confusedly, 'At least he's not marrying me for my money. My uncle left the cane farm to him, not to me.'

'Good God! And are you marrying *him* because of that?'

'Well, of course I'm not!' She sat back in her chair breathing quickly and glanced round with envy at all the other happy, relaxed diners. What an assumption to make! She felt both upset and angry. Marrying Clifford was—always had been—a dream come true. When you fall in love at fourteen and he waits for you and it all happens just as you've longed for it to happen—— She looked at Mike, her dark eyes resentful. 'Can't you get it into your head that I'm in love with him?'

'And have been since you were fourteen,' he said sardonically. 'The classic schoolgirl crush, in fact.'

'It's a little more than that,' she retorted furiously.

He produced cigarettes again and this time lit one. 'Have you proved it?'

'Well, haven't I? I've come up here to marry him.'

He slanted her a look, then turned to summon the waitress and ask for coffee, and when his attention returned to her Amy said, 'You go on as if it was unnatural to want to get married. What do you know about it, anyhow? *You're* not married.'

'My dear girl, I'm thirty-six and I'm a realist. I've given marriage, among numerous other things, a lot of thought.' He ashed his cigarette and narrowed his eyes. 'Which is more than you have, I'm inclined to think, and that's a great pity. For my own part, I've more than once reached the conclusion that I haven't yet met the woman for whom I'm prepared to disrupt my whole life.'

Amy swallowed a mouthful of the hot coffee that had been placed in front of her and tried to think of something to say. The whole conversation had become too much for her and she hated the feeling that she must justify herself. She had been very happy about wanting to marry Clifford, and now this *stranger* seemed intent on making her have doubts. But she didn't have any doubts and she wasn't going to be talked into having them. She looked up at him and said carefully, 'All right, you like to be free. I just happen to want to get married. To Clifford.'

'Oh, of course to Clifford. Who else?' He closed one eye and stared at her disconcertingly out of the other, then he said dismissively, 'Drink up your coffee and we'll go home. You can ring Clifford and have a long talk and forget I ever irritated you by trying to get you to do a little thinking for yourself.'

'I've been thinking for myself for years,' retorted Amy, not worrying much whether it was true or not. 'And I'm quite happy with the result.'

'Fine. Then there's no more to be said.'

After an infuriated look at him, she drank her coffee and got up from the table. She thought of using her lipstick, if only to assert herself, but somehow she didn't relish the idea of having him watch her—which he would, she was certain.

They walked all the way home without speaking.

There were no lights in the house, so Karen wasn't back. Mike followed her up the steps and unlocked the door and they both went inside.

'Thanks for the dinner,' she said rather belatedly. 'May I use the telephone now?'

'Go ahead,' he said. She turned away, then paused as he said, 'Just a minute, Amy.'

'What?' She glanced round and staggered as he pulled her into his arms and began to kiss her on the mouth. Sheer surprise was followed by shock, and she pressed her lips together hard and tried to struggle away from him.

'Don't fight me.' He lifted his mouth from hers just far enough to speak and she felt the warmth of his breath. 'Let your lips relax, Amy. Don't you even know enough to do that?' He kissed her again unhurriedly, his lips moving warm and persuasive against her own before settling firmly and asking for some response from her. She didn't give it. Her mouth was stiff, her teeth clamped together.

Mike let her go at last and looked down into her face assessingly as she wiped her mouth with the knuckles of one trembling hand.

'Why did you do that?' she panted indignantly.

'To teach you the feel of another man's lips. And because I've never tasted the mouth of a headmistress's niece before,' he said with a sardonic smile. 'Shall I tell you how they taste?' He paused and she said nothing but simply stared at him. 'Like raspberry syrup,' he said slowly and carefully. 'That, and nothing more ... My advice to you is not to get married yet, Amy. You're just not ready for it.'

'Because I don't happen to want to kiss *you*?' she spluttered, her cheeks hectic now, her voice shaking. 'I'm marrying *Clifford*, not you—thank heavens!'

'You can leave heaven right out of it. I haven't asked you. And I repeat what I said—you're not ready to marry Clifford or anyone else. If you looked a little harder you might see it for yourself and realise you've been manipulated ... In the meantime, get going and ring your fiancé.'

'You're horrible!' Amy snapped, her fists clenched. 'What are you implying—I've been manipulated? I— I haven't!'

His brows rose. 'Oh yes, you have. This marriage-to-be is well and truly tied up with your uncle's estate. I wouldn't be far wrong if I said it was more or less a condition to his leaving the farm to Clifford. Good God, if it's plain to me from the sketchy facts you've let drop, then surely you can see it. Or do you prefer not to?'

'I don't have to see it, because it's not true. Clifford and I—we happen to be in love.'

'Then that's just great,' he said. He had folded his arms across his chest and he looked at her impassively. 'We don't need to discuss it further.'

Amy turned away and found a sob in her throat. She swallowed it down and hated Mike Saunders. He was spoiling everything. She—Uncle Ralph—Clifford—all they wanted was——

She didn't finish the thought. She went into the sitting room and closed the door before she switched on the light. She didn't want Mike to hear her conversation with Clifford—to hear and to sneer.

She needn't have worried, not about that. Because as it happened she didn't have a conversation with Clifford.

A woman's voice answered the phone when she'd dialled the number, and it was so totally unexpected that after a frozen moment she put the receiver back on its cradle with a shaking hand. Then she stood where she was, feeling dazed.

Clifford lived alone now her uncle had died. They had never employed a housekeeper at the farm—and Clifford had never said he'd taken anyone on. He was a bad letter writer, it was true, but he would have told her that. He didn't have a mother—any sisters. Amy clenched and unclenched her hands and heard herself breathing as if she were in pain.

It seemed an eternity before it dawned on her what had happened, and then she almost laughed. Of course! She'd been in such a dither after that scene with Mike she had dialled the wrong number. She drew a deep breath and tried again, giving it her full attention this time. And the same voice answered.

'Who's—that?' Amy croaked out.

'It's Margaret Leslie here. Is that you, Glenys?'

Amy didn't answer—couldn't. Her senses were reeling and she was shaking as though she had a fever. She hung up and sank into the chair behind her and sat there staring at nothing. Margaret Leslie wasn't just a name; it was someone she knew very slightly. A smart woman of thirty or so who ran an exotic gift boutique in downtown Cairns. She lived with a man—or had. Amy didn't know his name, but she knew they weren't married. She knew too that Clifford had bought her perfume there—also an Indian silk scarf he had given her last Christmas. But what on earth was Margaret Leslie doing answering the telephone at the cane farm in Mossman? It was all completely incomprehensible. Amy put her hands over her eyes. She felt like running away somewhere, hiding her head, until it was all over and it was safe to come out—to look. Because——

She refused to follow her thoughts, dreading where they might lead her.

She heard the door open and took her hands quickly away from her face and pretended to be looking at her ring.

It was Mike, of course, and he asked briefly, 'Did you get through?'

'Yes, thank you.' She sent him a quick look, forced a smile.

'What's the plan now he knows his friends have left town? Is he coming to fetch you?'

She moistened her lips and shook her head. 'He can't—yet. He's—busy with the crush—really busy,' she improvised. 'I—I might see if I can get a lift, take a coach——'

He frowned. 'I'm afraid I can't offer to drive you up. I have to get back to Bangalo tomorrow night.'

She flushed. 'I wasn't expecting you to offer. Besides, with Clifford so busy I—I might stay in town a few days.'

He looked as if he thought her hopelessly indecisive, and she didn't wonder. 'Well, it's up to you,' he said. 'I can't make up your mind for you. I'll see you in the morning. Make sure you put the lights out before you go to bed, will you?'

'I'm going to bed now,' she said, getting up from the chair. 'You can put out the lights. Goodnight.' She walked out of the room without sending him another glance. It wasn't very polite, but then she wasn't feeling in the mood to be polite, not to anyone at all. She was shaken to her heart and illogically she felt that Mike Saunders was somehow partly to blame. He'd upset her even before this had happened.

She helped Karen with breakfast next morning. Someone—Karen or Mike—had been out and bought eggs, bread, butter, and there was coffee and powdered milk in the cupboard. Karen was full of her evening out over breakfast, and no questions were asked of Amy for some time. The Fiorenzas had heard from Sandro. He and Pauline had been in Naples where Pauline had had her handbag snatched—but fortunately Sandro had all the travellers cheques, so she had only lost a little money. Now they were on their way to Rome, and from there they meant to go to Florence. Sandro was thinking of buying into a leather goods business there.

'With Pauline's money, of course,' Mike commented grimly over his coffee cup. 'And knowing nothing at all about that sort of thing.'

'Yes, but Mike, Mrs Fiorenza's not going to encourage it. She's very worried really. She says Sandro's just not a businessman and—well, Pauline's not a businesswoman either, is she?'

That question didn't even warrant an answer. 'If Pauline hopes I'll buy some of her shares—or allow her to sell outside the family,' he said, flinging down his table napkin, 'then she's damned wrong. Losing her head over an immature boy—careering off to Italy. I'll fly over to Italy myself and put a stop to all this nonsense. Pauline may be twenty-four, but she's acting like a sixteen-year-old. Mrs Fiorenza had better let me know when she has an address.'

'She will, Mike,' Karen said placatingly. 'She's promised to keep in touch with me. She's no more pleased than you are, honestly. All she wants is for Sandro to come back home and work on the farm.'

'That's hardly likely to happen now he's married Pauline,' Mike bit out. He pushed his chair back and left the table abruptly, and as he disappeared, Karen sighed, 'Oh gosh, isn't he wild! I don't know what to think. I just wish Pauli hadn't married Sandro in the first place—she's really got herself into a mess.' She pushed her plate aside with a look of distaste. Obviously she was no more interested in breakfast than her brother was, and Amy made a rather gloomy third.

Presently Karen asked with an effort, 'Did you ring Clifford last night, Amy? I hope he's fixed up for you to go to Mossman. Mike's decided to fly back to Bangalo this evening, so he won't be staying here tonight.'

'That's all right,' said Amy. 'Actually I can't go to Mossman yet. There are a few things to be sorted out.'

She had decided not to tell Karen about that telephone call yet. After all, there might be some perfectly reasonable explanation for Margaret Leslie's presence in Clifford's house at that time of night—though what on earth it could possibly be she didn't know. She'd spent a wretched night thinking about it and the only conclusion she'd been able to reach was the obvious one—that Clifford was having an affair with another woman. Either that or he was in love with her. It didn't seem possible, yet she couldn't forget that remark of Mike's about deathbed promises—a guarantee of disaster if you hold each other to it.

Amy simply didn't know how to cope with the situation. She shouldn't have hung up last night, of course. She should have asked to speak to Clifford. After all, he hadn't said anything to her about wanting to end their engagement—he hadn't stopped her coming here, he'd only asked her couldn't she wait another week. So didn't that look as though she was in danger of jumping to the wrong conclusions? Just the same, Margaret Leslie was in Mossman, and Clifford thought *she* was safely taken care of in Cairns. For the first time she was really aware of her own lack of experience and she glanced at Karen wondering if she could help—and decided she couldn't.

'As a matter of fact,' she told Karen, 'Aunt Evelyn doesn't think I should stay alone in the house with Clifford, and the idea was for me to go to some people down the road. But they've had an influx of visitors, so I can't, and with Clifford so busy and the MacDonalds being away, everything's in a real mess. The fact is, I've picked the wrong time to come north. I can see that now. Clifford did ask me to wait, but I wouldn't, so it's all my own fault.'

Karen looked at her sympathetically.

'Is everything all right, Amy?'

'Of course. It's just that—that I've got some time to fill in.'

'Then why not come to Bangalo with us? It'd be fun, and you could stay just as long as you liked—till Clifford's free and there's somewhere for you to stay and so on.'

Amy felt tempted—and then she thought of Karen's brother and had second thoughts. 'It's not worth it, Karen. It might all be straightened out by tomorrow. But thanks all the same.'

'That's okay,' said Karen. 'But remember, Bangalo's there if you should want to come.'

The two girls did the washing up and then Amy went to her room to tidy up and to pack her things. She wished again that she had had the sense to speak to Clifford last night instead of losing her nerve so completely. Then she might know where she stood, and what to do. She would have to ring again tonight, that was all, and she dreaded the thought. Karen was going to spend the morning shopping, and that gave Amy a bright idea. She would go to Margaret Leslie's boutique and see what she could find out! Why not? A miracle might happen—she might discover her suspicions were absolutely baseless.

She *might*.

She put on a cool white dress with a split skirt, put sun-block on her face, grabbed a hat and sun-glasses and left the house with Karen. They parted at the shopping centre and Amy went straight to the gift boutique. The shop was busy as it always was—busy and crowded because it was rather small. Tourists were milling around looking for trophies for themselves or gifts for other people and it was five minutes before

Amy was able to speak to the pretty young assistant whom she had heard being addressed as Glenys. She wore a sarong and she was friendly and helpful, just as Amy had always found Margaret Leslie to be.

'Are you looking for something in particular or do you need some help?' Glenys asked with a smile.

'I was hoping to see Margaret Leslie, as a matter of fact,' Amy said glibly. 'Will she be in this morning?'

'I'm afraid not. She's on holiday just now. You're a friend of hers, are you?'

'Not, not exactly. She and her—er—friend knew my uncle,' Amy improvised, a little to her own horror. 'He died recently and I wanted to let them know. You couldn't tell me where she—they—either of them is, I suppose?'

Glenys looked at her with a mixture of sympathy and curiosity. 'I guess you're talking about Jim Garnett. They've split up, and I don't know where he is these days, but Margaret's staying with a friend in Mossman. She'll be back in the shop next week, as a matter of fact, so if you're staying in Cairns you could pop in next Monday and you'll be sure to catch her. She's usually in around ten or so.'

'Thanks very much,' Amy managed to say before she turned away and went into the street. She felt stunned. So Margaret would be back in a week—and hadn't Clifford urged her to wait another week before she came north? It was all pretty conclusive and it was very, very hard to take. She put on her sun-glasses and walked slowly along with the crowds thronging the footpath. She thought about Margaret and wondered what she had that she herself lacked. Maturity, for one thing. But she had been so sure that Clifford loved her —and Uncle Ralph must have thought so too, or he would never have urged them to marry. And Clifford had agreed so willingly.

Now what was she going to do? Invite disaster by holding him to his promise? Tell him she knew—accuse him? She couldn't see herself doing any of those things.

Somehow she found herself at a public telephone dialling his number again—knowing he would be in the canefield, knowing it would be Margaret Leslie who would answer, yet hoping and praying that she wouldn't.

'Hello?' Margaret Leslie said.

'Could I speak to Clifford North, please?' Amy hoped the nervous tremor in her voice wasn't obvious. She was trying very hard to be casual.

'Clifford's not in at the moment. Who's calling?'

'She knows,' Amy thought, some sixth sense telling her it was so. 'They've talked about me——'

'It's Amy Martin,' she said, and then her courage failed her. She couldn't ask who she was speaking to—she couldn't. She said hurriedly, 'Could you take a message, please? Would you let Clifford know that his friends in Cairns have gone away so I haven't been able to stay with them.'

'What? The MacDonalds?' The other woman's voice was sharp, and obviously she knew all about the arrangements for keeping Amy away from the cane farm.

'Yes. So I—I wondered if Clifford would like me to come up to Mossman on the coach.'

There was a moment's pause, then, 'I think you'd better talk to Cliff about that. Can he ring you tonight? Where are you staying?'

Where was she staying? Where would she be when *Cliff* told her it was all over? Alone in some motel room—— As though she were drowning she clutched at the memory of Karen and her invitation, swallowed hard and said firmly, 'I'll be at the Hotel Bangalo. He can ring me there. I'm going to stay with—friends.'

'I'll tell him. Goodbye.' A note of satisfaction, of finality, in the voice, and bang! the receiver was replaced and the conversation was over.

Amy was quivering. Margaret Leslie hadn't told her; it was up to Clifford to do that. Miserably, walking like a zombie, she made her way to a small café, bought herself a coffee and sat drinking it and staring into space. Wondering if she should simply pack up and go back to Sydney. To what? It was unbearable. To tears, and the wedding dress that wasn't quite finished. To explanations that would satisfy Aunt Evelyn—or wouldn't satisfy her. Incomplete explanations, because she hadn't even talked to Clifford. Nothing had been said, it was all guesswork on her part, though informed guesswork.

Another little fact clicked into place. That woman who had referred to Clifford as her cousin. Oh, dear God! Clifford should never have let her come. But he'd be feeling badly about it, of course.

She got herself a second cup of coffee and a new thought struck her. What if Clifford wasn't going to tell her it was all over, but was determined to keep his deathbed promise—so as not to hurt her, so as not to—to betray Uncle Ralph's trust in him? That was worse than anything. He would explain Margaret Leslie away and the marriage would go on—farcically—and it would be a disaster. Amy looked dry-eyed at her coffee, lifted the cup and could hardly swallow, she was so choked up inside.

It only she hadn't found out—if only she'd waited that week or two! Where ignorance is bliss——

Yet wouldn't the disaster still have been lurking in the background?

No, she wasn't going to run away to Sydney. Clifford would ring her tonight, and surely, surely there was still a chance it was all a nightmare she had dreamed up herself.

She left the rest of her coffee and went back to the Saunders' house. Karen was there already, fixing lunch. Mike, thank heaven, was not yet in.

'Hi!' Karen called through the house. 'Is that you, Amy? I'm concocting a salad, and I've made some alcohol-free punch. Come on out!'

'I'll be right there,' Amy called back. She went to her bedroom and pulled off her hat and ran her fingers through her hair before crossing to the mirror and picking up her comb. She was amazed to discover that her reflection looked no different from usual. She looked a bit smudgy under the eyes—that was her sleepless night—but otherwise she was perfectly normal. No one would guess to look at her that her whole world was as sure as sure about to be wiped out by a metaphorical cyclone.

She kicked off her sandals, tidied her hair, and retouched her lipstick—subtly pink with a hint of copper in it, as different as could be from the lush red she had worn last night when she went out with that awful Mike Saunders.

In the kitchen, she drank thirstily a whole tall glass of the fruit punch, then laid the table for two. Mike wouldn't be in to lunch, and that was the first good thing that had happened that day. While they ate a ham and pineapple salad, rather haphazardly put together—Karen was no wizard in the kitchen—Karen talked about the purchases she had made in town.

'Life's very informal on Bangalo. You need lots of cool simple cottons and Cairns is super for that kind of shopping. I'll show you what I bought after lunch. How did your morning go? Did you settle some accommodation for tonight?'

'Well, no,' Amy admitted. 'I—I rang Clifford again. It will be a few days before he's straightened things out. You know what you said about coming to Bangalo, Karen? I'd like to do that after all, if you're sure it will be all right.'

'Oh, great!' Karen was enthusiastic. 'You might as well enjoy yourself instead of mooning about on your own. You'll probably be able to stay in Mike's bungalow—that's where I'll be quartered, of course. I'll ask him when he comes in.'

Amy protested in vain, and predictably, when he came in at four, Mike was not enthusiastic. The two girls were lounging in the shade of the garden and he strode across to them.

'You still here?' he said to Amy, who wanted to answer with a smart and acrid, 'What do you think?' but under the circumstances didn't. He went straight to the fridge under the house and got himself a couple of cans of beer, then slung himself down in a chair, unbuttoning his shirt with the fingers of his free hand.

'I hope you're packed up, Karen. The minute I've drunk this we're moving. Do you want to be dropped off somewhere, Amy?'

Amy moistened her top lip nervously and wished she was independent after all.

'She's coming to Bangalo with us,' Karen said smoothly. 'There's room in the Cessna, isn't there, Mike?'

He took the beer can from his lips and narrowed his eyes to stare at Amy.

'What the hell's all this about? Why the change of plan? I thought the attraction as far as you're concerned was at Mossman, not on Bangalo Island.'

Amy gritted her teeth and Karen cut in again, 'Clifford's up to his neck in work, Mike, and I've persuaded her to come and visit us instead of putting in time all by herself in Cairns.'

'It's not a—a change of plan,' Amy explained, and knew the minute she'd said it that it was horribly untrue. All her plans looked like changing—from here to eternity. 'And don't worry, I won't thrust my company on you. You can just regard me as another holiday guest like anyone else.'

'Don't be crazy!' Karen exclaimed. 'You'll be our *personal* guest, won't she, Mike?'

Mike drained the last of his beer and got to his feet. 'Hotel guests make their bookings weeks ahead,' he said, ignoring Karen. 'Have you checked with the office to see if you can get a suite, by any chance?'

Amy blinked. 'No, not yet. But——'

'Well, it's too late now. But since Karen's invited you, you'd better come across with us and we'll see what can be done. Now get those glasses rinsed out. I expect to be on the way in twenty minutes.'

Karen made a face behind his back. 'Don't worry, Amy. He likes to throw his weight about, but why on earth did you have to talk about being a hotel guest when you know I didn't mean that?'

Amy shrugged. 'I'm sorry, Karen, but your brother seems to find me irritating. I'd much sooner do as I said, if it's possible.'

'Well, if it's not, Mike will just have to be a bit more civil,' Karen said heatedly. 'If I can't invite my friends to what's going to be my home, it's a pretty poor look-out. But don't look so glum—we won't argue about it, and I'm positive everything will be okay. Meanwhile we'd better get moving.'

Amy agreed. There was no point in deliberately goading anyone as autocratic as Mike Saunders.

CHAPTER THREE

LESS than an hour later the three of them, with Mike as pilot, were flying out from Cairns in the little four-seater Cessna Skylane. Amy had never been in such a small plane before, and despite everything she felt thrilled and excited, looking down on the sea so calm and clear and palely green, where small islands lay like scattered jewels, their shores scalloped with gold and silver sands.

When Karen exclaimed, 'There's Bangalo, Amy,' she stared down at the tiny island they were circling, discovering it looked totally uninhabited until one caught a glimpse of roofs through the thick green foliage of trees.

'If you're interested, Amy,' Mike remarked, 'Bangalo's a continental island, like a great many others of the islets in the Barrier Reef Channel. Can you see the fringe of coral round it through the water? And if you're thinking to yourself it's not as romantic as a true coral island, then believe me you're wrong. The vegetation's far more lush and varied, and we have a mountain in Bangalo you might like to climb. If you're here long enough,' he added.

His tone made Amy hope that she wouldn't be, but she murmured non-committally, and caught sight of the red ribbon of the tiny airfield as Mike turned the plane. The engine made a different sound, and only minutes later they touched down with scarcely a bump. 'I'd give him full marks for that,' she thought with approval, but kept it to herself.

The assistant manager from the hotel, Paul Richards, was waiting for them in a car. He was a good-looking, suntanned man, pretty close to forty, Amy guessed, as he left the car and came to help with the luggage, to greet Karen, shake hands with Mike, and be introduced to Amy—'Amy Martin, a friend of Karen's,' Mike said, and Amy felt she'd been brushed off as of no account, which, she supposed, was exactly what she was. But Paul's smile was warm and welcoming, and she felt a little comforted.

'Not been here before?' he asked as they went across to the car in the shade of the casuarinas. The evening sun was still hot but there was a cool breeze from the sea, and Amy guessed that the nights here would be a little cooler than they were in Cairns. 'You're going to love it. It's a great place for a holiday, and a great place to work. I've been here five years and I'm prepared to stay another twenty-five,' he finished with a smile, opening the car door for her.

The drive to the hotel complex was along a sandy road fringed with pandanus palms and casuarinas, and soon the hotel came into view. There were tall coconut palms, the spread of a tropical garden with cascading bougainvillea and huge red and yellow and pink hibiscus flowers. The guest suites were scattered through the garden and along by the beach, and centrally situated was the main hotel building—lounge, restaurant and reception, overlooking a terrace and swimming pool. When Paul pulled up they all got out of the car and while he unloaded the luggage, Mike said, 'I'll see if we have an empty suite, Amy,' and disappeared in the direction of reception.

'I hope we haven't,' said Karen. 'Our bungalow's round the far end of the beach, away from all this. It will be much nicer if you're there with us. Mike will behave himself, you'll see. I don't know what's got into him. He's generally really nice to my friends.'

Well, he hasn't been all that nice to me, Amy thought, and at that moment he came back.

'You can move into number five down near the beach, Amy. I hope that will suit you. Paul will have your luggage sent down, and Karen can show you where it is.' Without another word he strode away.

'Damn!' Karen exclaimed. 'You'll be miles away from us. Come along, anyhow.'

The suite Amy was to occupy consisted of a spacious room with two beds, plus a fair sized bathroom. A big fan was already whirring in the high ceiling, and wide glass doors, with sliding insect screens attached, opened on to a small private terrace, shaded by a sloping shingle roof. No more than a few feet away was the beach, framed by coconut palms. The sea had softened to creamy blue in the evening light, and out there she could see another small islet—probably a true coral cay, she thought—very tiny and looking like a dish piled high with greenery. It was beautiful—so beautiful, she thought with an ache in her heart, and remembered Karen's suggestion that she and Clifford should spend their honeymoon there. Now it didn't look as though there would be a honeymoon at all ...

'I'd better not ask you to have dinner with us,' Karen was saying. 'Mike will expect me to eat with the staff in the dining room—Pauli did, I know. No favouritism, that's the idea. Anyhow, I'll leave you to settle in. Dinner's on any time from seven on, and there's a bar in the lounge, if you're interested.' With a smile she was gone, and Amy was alone, with only her sore heart for company.

But that was infinitely preferable to sharing a bungalow with Mike Saunders.

Her baggage came, and she kicked off her sandals and felt the pleasant shock of the cool quarry tiles against the soles of her feet. She began to unpack, painfully aware of the fact that she had planned her wardrobe with Clifford in mind. Well, for goodness' sake, she told herself sternly, don't go into a decline yet— wait till he telephones. And that could be any time from now on, she realised, glancing at her watch. There was no telephone in her room, but an information brochure on the long table top of natural wood told her that there was a telephone service from the mainland from eight in the morning until nine-thirty at night. If Clifford rang, someone would come for her. But she decided she would let them know at Reception that she was expecting a call, and she would stay somewhere handy as long as she could.

She showered, got into an emerald green dress with shoe-string shoulder straps, and slipped her feet into black, bare-look sandals. She fastened green glass earrings in her ears, glanced in the mirror for reassurance, and left her suite. Outside it was almost dark, and a stream of hotel guests was heading for the restaurant. Low-set lights flowered in the garden, discreetly illuminating the paths, the coconut palms whispered and there was a heavenly scent of frangipani flowers in the air.

Along with her luggage had come a voucher for a complimentary drink—'Your first drink at the bar, Bangalo's own special cocktail, the Island Spell'. Amy was no drinker, and she couldn't imagine going alone to the bar anyhow—not even for a lemon squash. She was nervous enough about going to the restaurant alone, as a matter of fact.

She had almost reached Reception when someone caught her lightly by the arm, and she turned her head to find herself looking into the face of Mike Saunders. He wore black pants, and a black open-necked shirt, and he looked frighteningly familiar yet somehow strange as well.

'I called at your suite and found you'd gone,' he said almost curtly. 'Karen's eating with the staff——'

'I know,' Amy broke in. 'It doesn't matter. I can fend for myself as well as any girl holidaying on her own. I don't want to be a bother to you—I'm well aware I'm not exactly welcome.'

He didn't contradict her, but he said dryly, 'Most girls coming alone to a resort like this are looking for male company—a romance. Are you? If so, then go ahead, look after yourself.'

'I—of course I'm not looking for male company. But I don't want to eat with you.'

'I wasn't going to ask you to, honey,' he said with irritating superiority. 'I have other more important things to do right now. I merely thought I'd check if you'd like me to ask Caroline—our restaurant hostess— to put you at a table with someone you'll be safe and happy with. Otherwise, she's likely to fix you up in a group of unattached guys and girls. And with your attractions,' he added, his eyes assessing her clothes, her figure, 'someone's going to be chasing you along the beach at the first possible opportunity. And you'll have to run really fast if you don't want to be caught.'

'Don't be ridiculous,' Amy said coldly. 'I've never gone in for that sort of thing.'

'Well, I know that,' he drawled out. 'But okay, if

you want to go it alone, then carry on.'

'I will,' said Amy, glad he didn't know how hard her heart was hammering. 'Thank you for offering to come to the rescue, but whatever your opinion of me, I assure you I can manage perfectly without you.'

'Then that's fine.' He turned on his heel and left her and she continued on her way, going first to the reception desk about her phone call, then on to the restaurant.

As she stood waiting inside the restaurant entrance, a rather voluptuous young woman dressed in an exotic sarong floated towards her and asked with a bright smile, 'Are you on your own?'

'Yes,' Amy admitted. This must be Caroline, and rather helplessly she followed her, between the candle-lit tables, many of them already occupied. It was a big room with a high pine ceiling where several fans whirred. The top half of the walls was open, because the long shutters had been raised to let in the cool evening air. Waitresses, all of them young, all of them wearing sarongs with a hibiscus design, hurried to and fro, while wine waiters in their black pants and white shirts made a sober contrast.

Caroline, true to Mike's prediction, showed her to a table where there were two girls and three men, all of them youngish, and as she sat down she was conscious of being looked over by five pairs of eyes.

'Hi,' one of the girls said. 'I'm Barbara, and this is Kay.'

The boys announced themselves as Nev, Richard and Dave, and Amy said a general hello, and added, 'I'm Amy.'

One of the waitresses—Richard called her Susie with an easy familiarity—came and handed her a menu and she ordered a seafood platter and salad. She didn't feel terribly interested in food, she was too much on edge now waiting for Clifford's phone call, and she gave only part of her attention to the chatter and questions that flew back and forth at the table. Dave, who looked older than the other two boys and was certainly heftier, poured her a glass of wine, and by the time she had eaten what she could of her meal, she discovered she had somehow been teamed up with him. If Mike had thought it would worry her, he was quite wrong, because Dave was fairly unsophisticated and quite without guile. He was a sheep farmer from Victoria, and having, he said, a whacko time in the tropical north.

'Where are you from, Amy? The bush, same as me?'

'I'm from Sydney,' Amy told him, and moved her left hand on the table so that her ring would catch his eye—though it didn't.

'From Sydney? I'd never have guessed it. You look like a country girl, nice and fresh,' Dave commented, and Amy smiled palely and thought of Mike's remarks about raspberry syrup. At all events, she didn't think Dave was the type to chase her along the beach, though she wouldn't put that kind of thing past either Nev or Richard, who were far slicker. Anyhow, after dinner she was going to find a chair in the lounge as near as possible to Reception and wait there for her call. No one was going to have a chance to chase her along the beach!

But it wasn't as easy as all that. When they all got up to leave the table, Dave cast an admiring glance over her green dress and put an arm around her waist to guide her among the tables.

'Dancing doesn't start till eight-thirty,' he remarked. 'We can have a drink and a talk first.'

'Oh, I've had enough to drink,' Amy said, discon-

certed that he should take it for granted she was going
to spend the evening with him. 'Besides, I'm expecting
a telephone call any minute. From my fiancé,' she
added deliberately.

'Oh, now don't tell me you're engaged just when I
was counting myself in luck,' Dave exclaimed, and he
gave her waist a little squeeze.

Amy walked faster. 'Well, I am,' she asserted, and
with a little shock realised it was possibly no longer
true after all.

'I'll look after you while this bloke of yours isn't
around,' Dave suggested. 'How about that?'

Amy's heart sank. It wasn't going to be terribly easy
to get rid of Dave without being rude, but her mind
was made up; she was going to find that chair and wait
there till her phone call came. And another time she'd
be more careful whose table she shared.

As luck would have it, the other four had found a
low table surrounded by comfortable cane chairs with
squashy cushions in just the spot Amy would have
picked, and she and Dave joined them. The dance band
hadn't started up yet, but a white-haired suntanned
man of about sixty was playing the piano and it was
very pleasant. Amy sank back in her chair and listened,
and thought fleetingly of Pauline and her guitarist. She
was surprised when Dave suddenly appeared in front of
her with a glass goblet containing coffee, topped thickly
with cream.

'Here you are, beautiful—a Tia Maria coffee. You
look the kind of girl who'd prefer that to Irish.'

She took it from him, saying helplessly, 'You really
shouldn't have, Dave. I don't——'

'Oh, drink it up, Amy, you'll love it,' he said, sitting
down in the next chair.

Amy took a sip and found it sweet and very pleasant,

and she took another sip. Why, after all, should she sit round gloomily when Clifford was—was probably making love to another girl? The thought, coming unexpectedly into the open, sickened her and she drank more of the coffee, mainly to hide the tears that had rushed to her eyes. She pretended to listen to the conversation the others were having, but she didn't hear a word, and presently the band started to play and a few couples went on to the floor, including the other four with her and Dave.

Dave got up and held out his hand to her.

'Coming?'

Well, what was wrong with dancing with another man when your own fiancé was sharing his bed with another woman? Amy danced—and discovered that Dave's main idea when he got a girl on to the dance floor was to hold her as close as possible. When he put his lips against her hair, she pulled away from him.

'I'm going to see what's happened to my phone call,' she said abruptly, and whether he liked it or not she hurried off the floor and he followed her. And across the room she saw Mike Saunders, in his black pants and shirt, watching her sardonically.

A girl in a sarong came towards her. 'Miss Martin, could you take a phone call in Reception?'

With a sigh of relief and a murmured excuse, Amy headed for the office. Her throat was constricted now, and she completely forgot everything else as she lifted the receiver.

'Hello. Clifford?'

'Amy, is that you?'

The very sound of his voice made her legs turn to water, and she sank down weakly in a chair.

'What on earth are you doing on Bangalo Island?' Clifford demanded.

'Didn't M——' Amy stopped and started again. She didn't want to sound as if she were accusing him of something, by mentioning Margaret Leslie. She tried again and said stumblingly, 'Didn't the—the woman I spoke to yesterday give you my message—explain?'

'I got your message but no explanations,' said Clifford, without attempting to tell her who the woman was.

'Well, the MacDonalds weren't there.' Amy wished she hadn't drunk that coffee, she didn't seem able to think clearly. 'Their daughter's baby had arrived prematurely and they had to look after the other two children—in Townsville.'

'Then why couldn't you have stuck around in Cairns? There are lashings of motels there, and you're not hard up. Are you?'

'No.' Amy swallowed nervously. The way he was talking to her he sounded like an unsympathetic stranger. He was as bad as Mike Saunders—worse. She pulled herself together and said, 'No, I'm not hard up, Clifford, and that's why I decided to fly over to Bangalo. I'm with friends,' she finished.

'What friends?' he asked almost suspiciously, and she could hear the frown in his voice, see the tightening of his rather straight mouth.

Amy sighed. 'Does it matter? No one you know, Clifford.' As she spoke, she could hear a woman's voice saying something in the background, and then Clifford must have put his hand over the mouthpiece because she couldn't hear it any more. 'When am I going to see you?' she asked. The fact that he said nothing about Margaret Leslie made her nervous, but she couldn't possibly broach the subject herself. She didn't want to sound suspicious because after all she might be imagining it all.

'I don't know, Amy,' Clifford said. 'I've told you, I'm busy.' There was that voice again and this time Amy heard the words clearly, 'Tell her, Cliff, for heaven's sake!' She caught her lower lip between her teeth and waited for Clifford to tell her—something she had already more than half guessed. But raising his voice, he said, 'I have to go into Cairns in a couple of days' time. Can you come over and meet me there?'

'Yes,' she said slowly and tightly. 'When, Clifford? Exactly when?'

'In a day or two.' Again he covered the mouthpiece, and then he said, 'The day after tomorrow. I'll meet you in the restaurant at David Jones, at three o'clock. We can talk there.'

'All right,' said Amy. 'Don't you want me to go back with you to the cane farm, Clifford?' she asked rather pitifully.

'It's not a case of what I want, Amy,' he said irritably. 'I've explained that the Delucas can't put you up. But we can see each other.'

'All right,' she repeated brokenly. 'Then I'll see you the day after tomorrow. Goodbye, Clifford. Thanks for ringing.'

She hung up, murmured her thanks to the girl at the desk, and went blindly to the door. Outside was the warm romantic tropical night, the scent of flowers. Dance music drifted enticingly from the lounge, but for Amy it had no significance. 'The end,' she thought, walking blindly ahead. The day after tomorrow—that was when Clifford was going to tell her that it was all over, that he'd fallen in love with another woman. He could have written—he could have told her before and saved her coming all this way, saved her dreaming on—— He could have put an end, she thought muzzily, to her staring at the candles on the birthday cake. So—

where to from here? What did she do with her life now?

'Hey, Amy, aren't you coming back to have a dance?'

It was Dave, and right now the thought of dancing with him, of having him drool over her, hold her close, ply her with liquor, was quite unbearable.

'I don't feel like dancing, Dave,' she said politely. 'I'm going back to my suite.'

'I'll come with you,' he said. He put his arm around her waist and hugged her. He had the strength of an ox, she thought, a little alarmed. He might be an unsophisticated countryman—'thick', someone like Karen would have called him—but he was the same as any other male. He was having a holiday, and girls were a part of it.

'I don't want you to come with me,' she said. 'I'm tired and I'm going to bed.'

'I'll come and soothe your fevered brow.'

'No, you won't——'

'Well, let's just stroll along the beach for a while.'

Amy tried to pull away from him, but his strength was too much for her, and she didn't know what she was going to do apart from making a scene, which wouldn't be very pleasant for anyone.

'Miss Martin,' someone said in a clipped voice.

It was Mike Saunders. Dave relaxed his hold and she half stumbled as she moved away from him. 'Excuse me,' said Mike with cool affability to Dave. 'I must have a word with Miss Martin.'

'Okeydoke,' shrugged Dave, evidently recognising Mike. 'I'll see you later on Amy.'

'Not—tonight,' she said shakily.

'Tomorrow, then? How about coming on the launch picnic to Dixon Island?'

'I don't think so, thank you,' she said shortly, and Mike took her arm and they walked in the direction of her lodge.

'Thank you for coming to the rescue,' she said when they had gone a few yards. 'I'm quite all right now.' She spoke coolly, distantly, but all the same she was grateful to him. It was just maddening to know that he'd warned her—offered help and she'd refused—and now she had had to let him extricate her from trouble.

Rather surprisingly, he didn't point it up or say, 'I told you so', but he did insist on accompanying her all the way to her suite.

'You didn't lock your door,' he remarked as she slid the insect screen across.

'No.'

'You'd better do that when you go inside.'

She didn't ask why, she just nodded. Everything seemed to be mounting up on her all of a sudden— the drink, Dave, the telephone call. Even Mike coming to the rescue. In a moment she was going to burst into tears.

'Goodnight,' she muttered, and as she went to slip inside her room he caught her by the hand and held it fast in his own.

'What's the matter?' he asked roughly.

'Nothing,' she said in a choked voice, not looking at him. And then to her dismay she did burst into tears. Before she knew what was happening he had thrust her into the room, followed her, pulled the long curtains across, and switched on the wall light that was little more than a night lamp. Amy put her head down and looked for a tissue in her purse.

'You'd better tell me about it,' said Mike through his teeth, and she thought what a nuisance she was.

'About *what*?'

'You had a phone call, didn't you? From your fiancé?'

'Yes.'

'Well then, let's hear the sad story.'

'There's—there's no sad story. I'm going to meet him in Cairns the day after tomorrow.'

'And you're crying about that?'

She glanced up and she thought Mike looked oddly menacing, standing there in his black clothes, one hand resting against the wall.

'I'm—I'm just in a silly mood,' she said huskily. 'Dave—upset me, and—I suppose I've had too much to drink.' She had found a tissue and she dried her eyes and blew her nose. Mike moved away from the wall and came nearer to her and she watched him uneasily.

'I don't believe you've had all that much to drink, Amy,' he remarked. 'But if you're in a silly mood——'

Without warning he took her into his arms and was kissing her. Her lips were warm, soft and unresisting against his own, but this was mostly because she was crying again. He kissed her gently, his lips moving to the corner of her mouth and then to her eyelids and her wet lashes, and she stood against him helplessly, clinging to him a little and wanting to cry and cry— but not till he'd gone.

'Is that better?' he asked her finally, holding her from him and looking down at her with faint mockery so that she felt like a child who was being comforted. She felt ashamed as well. It was so female—so weak and illogical to cry. What good were her tears going to do? Her fiancé was about to give her the bad news that the engagement was over—and she had a day and a half to brace herself ready for it. It wasn't going to kill her. She'd go on living. She'd even—probably—

eventually find somebody else. But not for a long long time, she thought.

She said flatly, 'I'm going to bed.'

'Do that. Shall I stay with you for a while?'

She looked at him, shocked. His eyes were enigmatic, and suddenly she knew she must look quite a fright with her tear-stained face and her messed-up make-up. If he stayed, it would be to pat her on the head and laugh at her inwardly.

'You—you think I'm a child, don't you?' she said resentfully. 'Raspberry syrup and birthday parties——'

He said, 'Sure. Kids cry at birthday parties when they're over-excited, and they drip tears into their raspberry syrup. And they respond to being kissed better and cuddled and humoured.'

'You've humoured me all you're going to,' she said. 'You can—you can go and look after somebody else now.' It sounded, the way she said it, ungracious, and that was how she felt. She didn't want Mike to get the wrong idea about the effect his kisses had on her. She saw his mouth twist sardonically.

'All right. And by the way, Amy, if you're going to Cairns in a couple of days and want a lift, I'll be flying across.'

'Not for my benefit, I hope,' she said antagonistically.

'Certainly not for your benefit. Merely by a lucky coincidence. Lucky for you, I mean,' he added deliberately. 'Well—goodnight.'

Amy didn't answer. She didn't even know when he'd gone. But after a few minutes she locked the screen door and spent half an hour messing around and settling herself in—taking a shower, brushing her hair, sniffing back a few tears now and again.

Then with the lights switched off, she looked out

into the night—the lovely starlit night, the shadows of the palms, the glint on the water. Bangalo Island, she thought, a tropical paradise where people like Kay and Barbara—and Dave—came to make a dream come true, for just a little while.

Where Amy Martin came when she woke up and found her dream had vanished ...

CHAPTER FOUR

THE next day Amy told herself she was beginning to accept what was inevitable. But she didn't need Dave or anyone else to help the process along.

She breakfasted in the restaurant, serving herself with fruit juice, pawpaw and pineapple, toast and coffee, and sitting alone at a table that overlooked the swimming pool and terrace. Her eyes were dry this morning, but she was dead inside. Well, almost dead. Just today to live through, and then the big scene.

She'd nearly finished eating when Karen came to the restaurant to find her.

'Hi, Amy! Did you sleep well? I'm off between ten and eleven this morning, so if you're not doing anything in particular you might like to come around to Coconut Beach and take a swim.'

Amy gave her a particularly bright smile, wondering if Mike had told her she'd been upset after her phone call, and hoping he hadn't.

'I'm not booked up. It would suit me fine.'

'Good. Then I'll drop by when I'm through. I'd better get back to work now before I'm reported absent!' Karen finished with a grin.

Amy finished her breakfast feeling a little more cheerful. When she went back to her lodge the bed had been made, there were fresh towels and everything was clean and tidy. She hoped Dave wouldn't turn up and try to persuade her to go for the launch picnic, and as he didn't she concluded—and hoped—he'd found himself another girl-friend. At ten o'clock Karen arrived, wearing a brief blue towelling playsuit. Amy had got into her maillot—yellow, sleek-fitting, covering her full breasts decently enough despite its plunging neckline, but revealing her waist, with its cut-out sides. On top of it she wore a long cotton shirt, and she slipped into thongs and set off with Karen along the path by the beach. Where the hotel beach ended, they cut through the tangle of pandanus palms and tea trees that covered a rocky point and emerged at another beach, small, curving, dominated by coconut palms.

'Our private beach,' Karen explained. 'You can see our bungalow through the trees. Nobody swims here but us, so you can swim topless—or completely in the nuddy if you like.' As she spoke, she unzipped her playsuit, revealing a pretty figure, not as full as Amy's, and a brief blue bikini. Amy peeled off her shirt, answering Karen only with a smile. She certainly wasn't going to bathe in the nude even if they did have the beautiful hot white beach all to themselves—at the moment!

They both went into the water and it was warm and clear and very still. They swam lazily for a while, and Amy refused to think or to do anything at all but enjoy the moment. As they left the water together, Karen remarked, 'Mike says you're going across to Cairns tomorrow to meet Clifford. Does that mean you're leaving us?'

'Oh no, I'll be back. Clifford's still up to his eyes in work. He can only spare me an hour or so because he—

he has some business in town. I'll have to keep out of
the way a little longer, at least.'

'Well, it may be selfish of me, but I'm glad we're
going to see more of you,' said Karen with a smile.

They sunbathed for a while, and then Karen had to
go—it was time to return to work. For a while Amy
stayed where she was, lying on the sand, and then she
sat up and hugged her knees. You could go just so long
without thinking, and then it all began to come back—
the hurt, the heartache——

It had all come back when Mike Saunders appeared.

He didn't seem in the least surprised to find her
there, in fact he seemed almost to be expecting it, but
she didn't know that he was very pleased. After all, it
was his private beach. Still, Karen had invited her here,
and she wasn't going to apologise or rush away.

'How are you this morning?' he asked curtly.

'Fine.'

'I'm glad to hear it.' He flung his towel down on the
sand near her and went into the water, where he swam
rather energetically, but with a smooth stroke that
scarcely disturbed the surface. Amy watched him, con-
centrating on doing that so as to escape following her
earlier train of thought.

When he emerged his eyes were reddish from the
salt water, and with his hair dark and sleeked down and
wet he looked vaguely different. His torso above brief
black swimming trunks was golden-brown and almost
free of hair—different from Clifford, who had a mass
of dark hair on his chest. Yet Mike was quite as masculine. More so, in fact, she found herself thinking.

He sprawled out near her on the sand and asked,
'Enjoying yourself?'

Well, for heaven's sake, after seeing her bawling last
night, did he really think she was enjoying herself?

She tried to decide between saying, 'Madly', and 'I'll give you one guess', but had said neither when he remarked, 'Okay, so you're not ... What time do you want to go to Cairns tomorrow?'

'I'm meeting Clifford at three,' she said. 'But you don't have to take me. I suppose there's a launch—or a plane——'

'There's a boat at ten,' he agreed. 'And Bush Pilots have a flight out at about one-thirty. Are you planning to check out?'

She moistened her lips nervously and hugged her knees closer to her. 'Do I—have to? I mean, is the suite I'm in booked up after tomorrow?'

'Luckily for you, no. You can stay on if you wish to.'

'Then I'll come back. Clifford's busy. We're just—just meeting, really.'

'To talk about the wedding?' he suggested mockingly.

'Yes.' Oh yes, to talk about the wedding, she thought bitterly. Clifford was going to tell her it was off. She twirled her engagement ring round on her finger in an absentminded way, and then thought, 'I'll have to give that back tomorrow'. That made it all seem terribly real, terribly final. But you couldn't keep someone's ring when they no longer loved you. And Clifford— well, there was Margaret Leslie ...

'Still determined to rush ahead and make plans?' Mike looked at her along one muscular, bronzed shoulder, salt and sea-water glinting on the points of his lashes. 'I hoped I might have persuaded you to think a bit harder about it all.'

'What?' She stared at him incredulously. 'You thought *you* might have persuaded me? How? How on earth do you imagine *you* could have done that?'

He shrugged and looked away from her at the peaceful shimmer of the pale water. 'In various ways. How-ever'—his glance came back to her—'if you're deter-mined to hang on to your golden dreams—your beau ideal, however outdated—when it's perfectly obvious even to a stranger like me that you're about to plunge into a soulless, arranged marriage—well then, by rights you should be allowed to drown in your own saliva, so to speak.'

Amy took a deep breath. She felt like throwing a handful of sand at him. If she had any sense at all, she'd get up and walk away, but he infuriated her so much she just had to answer back. The awful thing was, she was beginning to see he was probably right. It *was* an arranged marriage. Uncle Ralph had wanted it, she had wanted it. And Clifford—had he felt obliged to comply, seeing the property was going to be left to him? Amy was amazed she hadn't wondered about that before. But quite simply, she hadn't. Quite simply she'd believed her dreams were coming true. And now Clifford had fallen in love with someone else. She felt a pain in her heart, as if she had been wounded there.

She bit out angrily, painfully, 'You—you can think what you like, I don't care, I don't want to know. And I don't want to talk about it. To you,' she finished succinctly.

'To me or to anyone else,' he amended. 'Well, it seems talk's futile in your case.'

'Yes, it is,' she said furiously. 'I'm—I'm going,' she added, and scrambled to her feet. As she did so, he reached out suddenly and caught her by the ankle so that she fell back on the sand, with a gasp of shock. Before she could recover herself, his arms were around her and they were wrestling together. She felt the smoothness of his sun-warmed chest against her body, felt his bare strong legs tangling with her own. She heard herself panting as she somehow dragged one arm free of his grasp and scratched him viciously down the side of the neck.

In an instant she was free and she rolled away and sat up in the sand and stared at him with hatred.

He sat up too, his fingers going to his neck where small drops of blood glistened.

'I wouldn't want to be Clifford on your wedding night,' he remarked dryly. 'A little bit of sex quite definitely doesn't turn you on, does it?'

'Sex?' she repeated, quivering. 'Is that what you call it? I—I'd call it assault!'

'You would,' he said, unmoved.

'Yes, I would.' She reached for her shirt and put it on, and this time when she got to her feet he left her alone, and she walked away quickly.

Back at the hotel she showered and dressed in a wrap-around skirt and sleeveless top and went to the restaurant for lunch. It was a luscious-looking smorgasbord, and it was funny, but she felt hungry—really hungry. She helped herself lavishly to cold meats and salads and took her piled-up plate to a table occupied by a married couple and a child of about four. They turned out to be Americans from California, very friendly, very interested to hear about her, particularly when they knew her uncle had owned a sugar cane farm. Amy ate hungrily and answered their questions and forgot everything else. Everything, including Clifford—and Mike Saunders.

She spent the afternoon at the hotel pool. She didn't see Dave, who had probably gone on the barbecue picnic he'd mentioned. She swam, and then sunbathed, lying comfortably on a beach lounger under the palms. She had a magazine and sun-glasses and nobody bothered her. Occasionally she caught herself wondering where Mike was and what he was doing, but never once did she think of Clifford. Yet, oddly, she did think in a vague sort of way of tomorrow—of flying over to the mainland with Mike. It was lucky he was going to Cairns on that particular day.

Late in the afternoon Karen joined her at the pool.

'Having a nice lazy time?'

'Yes, I am. And you've been working!'

'Well, I love it. And don't you think Paul Richards is a peach?' Karen added, lowering her voice.

Amy agreed, though she hadn't given it much thought. 'Is he married?'

'A widower,' said Karen. 'I do like experienced men. They really know how to look after you—to make you feel good. Would you say Clifford is experienced?'

'Well——' Amy dragged her thoughts to Clifford with an effort. 'Well, yes, I suppose he is.' By now, at any rate, she thought. After a few weeks of Margaret Leslie's company in the house. Oh dear, yes, he was bound to be experienced.

'Did you see Mike this morning?' Karen asked inconsequentially.

Amy pulled her hat a little further over her eyes. 'Yes. He came to the beach before I left. I—I haven't seen him this afternoon though,' she added quickly as though to hide the thought of what had happened in the morning.

'I guess you haven't. He went out in the launch.'

'To Dixon Island? To the picnic?' Amy asked, surprised.

'Good lord, no. He went in his own boat—to see his girl-friend on Nerina Island.'

Amy's heart gave an unexpected lurch. His girl-friend! She hadn't known there was anyone in particular.

'She's rather a terrific girl,' Karen went on, leaning back and staring up at the blue sky through the palm fronds. 'Married—but she hasn't lived with her husband for about a year, so I expect she's in line for a divorce. A year's separation—that's all that's necessary. And irretrievable breakdown of the marriage, of course.'

'Oh. What does she do on this island—Nerina Island?' Amy felt somehow compelled to ask even while she was telling herself she didn't care a hoot.

'She's a painter. You may have heard of her— Delona Ferguson. She was written up in Pol a few months ago when she had an exhibition in Sydney.'

Amy shook her head. 'I've never heard of her. But then I didn't get round to many of the galleries.'

'Well, we'll get Mike to take us over to Nerina one day—if I can get off for a few hours,' said Karen. 'And I'll tell you what would be a super idea—if you like her paintings, I'll give you one as a wedding present.'

Amy was embarrassed. It was strange how quickly she had become accustomed to the idea that there was going to be no wedding—and hence no wedding presents, and she protested, 'No, honestly, Karen. She probably charges the earth.'

'Do you think that matters? I'm a Saunders, you know,' Karen said with a smile. 'And I hope,' she added after an instant, 'that Mike isn't going to get all ferocious and full of suspicion if Paul should happen to pay me a bit of attention. He's going to visit the Fiorenzas when he goes to Cairns tomorrow—he wants to track Pauline down as soon as he can. I wouldn't mind betting he'll be over in Italy in a week or so if he gets an address.'

'Really? What do you think he's going to do?' From what she knew about Mike, Amy could picture him carrying his sister off forcibly if necessary, and leaving her young gold-digging husband stranded in Italy.

'I haven't a clue,' shrugged Karen. 'But you know, much as I like the Fiorenzas, I really do wish Pauli hadn't married Sandro. He's got nothing to offer her and he hasn't even made up his mind what he wants to do with his life. He's'—she waved one hand in the air—'he's just hopelessly immature.'

'Like me,' Amy thought. 'Up to a point.'

'Do you think Mike will make Pauline come home?' she asked.

'He might. And Sandro too, so he can keep an eye on them. In which case, he'd do what he could to help, provided they pulled their weight. But Sandro—well, he's bigheaded in a way. Terribly good-looking, and he has this really sexy voice. But he's had no training. It's all such a shame,' Karen mused. 'You meet such masses of people in a place like this, and Pauline had to go and fall for Sandro.'

At that point Paul Richards came to join them, and after Amy had given a few polite answers to his enquiries as to how she was enjoying herself, she made her apologies and stood up, ready to go.

'Hang on a moment,' said Karen. 'I'm going over to the dance in the lounge tonight. Shall I see you there?'

'I'd like that,' Amy agreed. 'At eight-thirty?'

'On the dot.'

They smiled at each other and Amy made her departure. It was too early to dress for dinner, so she sat out on her little terrace. It was very pleasant and very quiet. Most of the hotel guests were swimming or playing tennis or picnicking, or had gone out to the reef to fish or to look at the coral. Her thoughts wandered to Delona Ferguson—Mike Saunders' girl-friend. Amy wasn't sure whether she wanted to visit her on her island or not. Mike was there now, and she hardly thought he'd be back for the dance tonight. He'd stay there, she thought. He was a—sexy man. She relived that mad scuffle on the beach, and felt indignant with him all over again. How dared he do that?—as if she were the kind of girl who enjoyed that kind of a skirmish! Yet she had a curious idea that he hadn't meant anything to happen more than had actually happened. If he had, then she wouldn't have escaped him nearly so easily. He'd been making fun of her again, probably, pointing up the fact that she wasn't—according to him —ready for marriage. And maybe he was right. She was too immature, too inexperienced. She'd never really thought what it would be like to have Clifford take possession of her body. But now——

Suddenly she got up and went inside. It was time to get ready for dinner.

She was right, she discovered that night. Mike didn't appear in the lounge.

She had shared a table at dinner with the American couple, Pat and Ray, and waved across the room to the others she had met the previous night. There was another girl at their table now, and Dave was busy paying attention to her, somewhat to Amy's amusement—and relief.

Afterwards in the lounge, the skipper of the hotel launch, a red-haired man called Steve, made a foursome with Karen, Paul and herself. She had several dances and was introduced to Con, the bandleader. She drank orange juice with the merest drop of vodka in it, and to a certain extent she enjoyed the evening. As far as she was concerned, the most awkward fact was that Karen made quite a thing of her being engaged and on the point of being married. When Steve quizzed her as they danced, she parried his questions and switched the conversation to him, and discovered he was married with two little girls, and that his wife was expecting another baby.

At eleven o'clock, Mike came into the lounge. Amy was aware of it instantly, mainly because so many heads turned in his direction—all of them female. A big broad-shouldered man, handsome and totally masculine and with a vitality about him that was formidable. Karen was dancing with Paul, and Amy, sitting at a low table with Steve, was sipping her second—and last, she decided—vodka and orange.

'The boss,' said Steve, following her glance, and she flushed and returned her attention to him.

'When the others come back, I think I'll go to bed. The island air makes me sleepy!' she told him.

Paul and Karen came back no more than a minute later, but she didn't go right away. She hadn't finished her drink, and while the others talked, Amy watched Mike covertly. He had taken a pretty girl on to the floor to dance. Very pretty and very sophisticated, though she looked to be in her early twenties. She had such poise and self-assurance as she laughed up at him that Amy thought she could have been a budding television star. She watched them dance, and as he looked down at his partner, Mike's face wore a look she had become familiar with—lazy, laconic, a mixture of tolerance and boredom in the half smile on his mobile mouth. He danced with the minimum of movement as though all his attention was focussed on the girl, and he was only on the dance floor at all because she expected it of him.

When the music stopped, she met his eyes quite unexpectedly across the room, and some passion flared in her. She thought with an intensity that was devastating, 'He won't dance with *me*, of course.' She looked away from him instantly without smiling and gave her attention to what the others were saying—though actually she didn't take in a word of it. And she sipped her drink slowly, because when it was finished she was going to bed.

When at last she set her glass down on the table, Steve glanced at her. 'Finished your drink, Amy? Like one more before you toddle off to bed?'

She hesitated, then said, 'No, thank you,' and smiled round at the others. 'If you'll excuse me——'

'Goodnight,' they all said, and up till the last minute she managed to refrain from looking for Mike. Then as she got up she glanced swiftly round the room, and discovered him at the bar. With a different girl now. Well, of course she'd been right. He wouldn't ask Amy Martin to dance.

She left the lounge quickly and went to her lodge.

She flew across to the mainland with Mike after lunch next day, and knew that she'd probably be late for her appointment with Clifford.

'No luggage?' he queried when they met outside Reception where one of the young hotel employees waited with a car.

'No,' she said, uneasy at once. 'But—but you said it would be all right for me to stay on.'

'Sure. I thought you might have changed your mind, that's all. I suspected you might be hoping to persuade Clifford to take you back to the farm despite all the gruesome pressure of work.'

She bit her lip at something in his tone, and got quickly into the car. He didn't believe Clifford was too busy for her to go there. And no wonder, because it certainly wasn't anything like the whole of the truth. She would have liked to say something to put him in his place, but he got into the front seat with the driver, leaving her in solitary splendour in the back.

It was too late for a retort once they were in the Cessna, and sitting beside him she saw the scratch marks she'd made on the side of his neck, blushed fiercely and turned away. Nevertheless, she enjoyed the lift into the air, the thrill of looking down on the tiny island and the clear beautiful colour of the sea. It was not till they came down at the airport in Cairns that she remarked doggedly, and really rather futilely when she came to think of it, 'I know you think it's funny about Clifford not taking me back to the cane farm, but I didn't explain it all to you——'

'Good God, Amy, you don't have to explain anything to me,' he said indifferently, and strode off. Infuriated, she had to almost run to keep pace with him as he headed for his car. He had explained to her that he had an engagement with a garage in Cairns to drive it back to town and bring it out to the airport when he needed it.

Once in the car, Amy started talking again—obstinately. 'I was supposed to stay with some friends of Clifford's, but they had unexpected guests, so——'

'So you were stranded? Just as you were stranded when the MacDonalds weren't at home. Okay, you can explain till the top of your head lifts off, Amy, but what's wrong with your going to your fiancé's home and staying there? Or does he only have one bed?'

Her face flamed. 'Of course not! There are three bedrooms. But——'

He was driving furiously fast into town, and when she paused he put in bitingly. 'But a good little girl doesn't shack up with a man—not even a man she's on the point of marrying. Sure, I know, Amy, I know. It might take the shine off your eyes, mightn't it? ... So now where would you like me to drop you off? I'm going out of town.'

'Anywhere,' she said stiffly.

He didn't argue. 'All right, I'll let you out at the Civic Centre. I'm going out along the Bruce Highway. And presuming you want to come back with me, I'll pick you up at the same place about five-thirty. If you're not there, I'll carry on without you, and it will be up to your fiancé to dispose of your body.'

'Thank you. I can hardly wait to see you again,' she said with angry sarcasm.

He smiled maddeningly. 'I'll look forward to hearing the result of your momentous meeting. Keep in mind what I've said when you're picking your wedding date, won't you? I'd suggest maybe five years hence—a nice long engagement in the good old-fashioned way. By then you just possibly might have grown up and discovered what it's all about.' He pulled up at the footpath as he spoke, reached across and opened the door, and she slithered out.

If he only knew, her wedding date was not anything like as close as five years hence. It was never. She slammed the door shut and turned her back on him, and suddenly discovered her legs were shaking. Because of him? Or because in a few minutes' time she would be seeing Clifford? She wasn't altogether sure, but as she was fifteen minutes late already, she began to walk quickly along the street in the direction of David Jones' store—where she was to meet Clifford in the cafeteria. Hardly romantic, and hardly private, and she wondered he couldn't have suggested a better place. But perhaps once they had had a coffee, they would walk down to the Esplanade. So he could break the news to her discreetly.

She saw Clifford the minute she went into the

cafeteria, and for an instant she stood stock still, staring at him as if he were a stranger. He was smoking, and he didn't look a bit happy. Poor Clifford! He must be feeling as badly as she did. He didn't want to hurt her. She remembered that voice on the phone insisting, 'Tell her, Cliff—for heaven's sake', and he'd refused; he'd wanted to tell her privately, to break it gently, she supposed.

She moved forward unwillingly.

'Clifford——'

'Amy!' He stood up and they smiled at each other, and Amy wondered anxiously if she should expect him to kiss her—now. He did—on her cheek. Not as he usually did, softly on her mouth.

'You're late,' he remarked, stubbing out his cigarette in the glass ashtray. I'd begun to think you weren't coming.'

'Sorry,' she said, sitting down and wondering if that was why he'd been looking so worried and unhappy. 'I couldn't time it exactly. You know—coming over from the island with friends.'

'Never mind,' he said abstractedly. 'Coffee?'

'Yes, please. And—and a cake, I suppose,' she added because he would expect her to eat something, though she wasn't feeling hungry.

His smile was not quite a smile, but he went to the counter and came back with two cups of coffee and some cake for her. Chocolate cake, thickly iced, and with cream in the middle. But no candles, she thought ridiculously.

'I'm afraid this has all been a big disappointment for you,' said Clifford as he sat down opposite her. He had hazel eyes, and she was baffled as she looked into them briefly. It was months since they'd seen each other, of course—and this was a crazy way to meet, under the circumstances. More than ever she felt he was a stranger.

'It's all my own fault,' she said awkwardly. 'Rushing up here without giving you enough time to—to arrange anything——'

'Yes. Well——' He stirred his coffee. 'We *had* decided to give it a year, after all.'

Amy began to eat her cake, her eyes downcast. She waited for him to go on, to say, 'I'm afraid I've fallen in love with someone else,' but he didn't say it.

'I don't want you to make a mistake,' he said, instead. 'I'm very fond of you, you know, Amy—I always have been since you were a kid.'

Amy wanted to laugh—but bitterly. The man she'd promised to marry telling her he was very fond of her! What would Karen think if she could hear that? What would Mike Saunders make of this—this heady, passionate conversation, over chocolate cream cake and coffee?

Clifford pushed his cup aside, his coffee only partly drunk, and Amy took another mouthful of cake and wondered if she was going to be able to swallow it.

'Do you mind if I smoke?' Clifford asked.

'Of course not, Clifford. Go right ahead.'

He lit a cigarette and drew on it and said nothing, and she felt nervous on his behalf. It was an awful thing to have to tell someone who loved you that it was all over. She could see so clearly that he didn't want to do it, that he didn't want to hurt her, but it had to be done, so she gave him a lead.

'Your housekeeper, Clifford—the woman I spoke to on the phone—does she—er—live in?'

She looked at him as she spoke, her dark eyes

troubled, and he raised his lids to give her one quick look, then flicked them down again and ashed his cigarette.

'She lives in Mossman,' he said stiffly. 'Comes in a few times a week.'

'Oh, Clifford,' she thought sadly. 'That's not true—why don't you say it?—get it over?'

'I'm going to say something you won't like much, Amy,' he was hurrying on. 'I think you should go back to Sydney and see the year out as we'd decided. I—I don't like making carefully thought out plans and then going mad and discarding them.'

Amy looked at him steadily. 'Was that what you wanted to talk about, Clifford? About my going back to Sydney?'

He ran his fingers through his dark hair and she saw he was sweating slightly. He was really upset about this, and he said finally, 'As a matter of fact, yes. I know you probably won't agree, but believe me, it's the best thing to do.'

Her eyes were quizzical. 'You don't want to get married so soon? You—you think we might have second thoughts about each other?'

He looked a little relieved. 'It does happen, Amy. The thing is, you're so young, and if you try to look at it reasonably, you'll see your uncle more or less pushed us—you, I mean—into this engagement.'

'Yes, I have begun to see that,' Amy said slowly—but it was Clifford who had been pushed into the engagement, not herself. She waited, but he didn't even hint that he had found somebody else, and after a moment she asked thoughtfully, 'If I met someone else—fell in love with another man—what would you do, Clifford?'

He gave her a quick look of surprise. 'I'd release you,

of course.' He drummed his fingers moodily on the table, but he didn't ask, as she had thought he would, what *she* would do if he fell in love with another girl. But of course that would be different. She saw it with a sudden awful clarity. *He* was the one who had the cane farm—which Uncle Ralph had quite plainly meant them to own jointly. *She* could change her mind with impunity, but he couldn't. And it really wasn't his fault if he preferred another woman to her.

Oh, how she wished her uncle had arranged things differently, so that each of them would have been independent of the other! It was not that she begrudged Clifford the farm, but she realised it had put him in a compromising position. It was exactly as she reached that point in her reflections that a brilliant idea came into her mind. Or at least, it seemed brilliant at the time. It was the one and only way to free Clifford painlessly—to absolve him of his guilt, to solve his dilemma. 'I'd release you,' he'd said, 'if you fell in love with someone else ...'

She said slowly, nervously, into the rather unhappy silence that had fallen between them, 'As a matter of fact I—I have something to tell you, Clifford. I hope you won't be too hurt, but—but I *have* met someone else. And it's serious,' she added, so that there should be no doubt. 'He—he wants to marry me.'

'What?' Clifford stared at her unbelievingly. 'You've met someone else? Well, good lord above, Amy, why didn't you come out with it long ago, instead of shilly-shallying around?' The relief in his voice was plain. It shone from his eyes and she thought more than a little bitterly how differently she had reacted when she had found out about Margaret. He was even laughing a little, and now that his face was animated he looked much more like the Clifford she used to know, the

Clifford she had been so mad about. 'Who is it, Amy? Who have you lost your heart to? That geology teacher?'

Who? Amy's mind went blank. Clifford was joking about the geology teacher, who had been married, anyhow. It was all very well to make a statement—a positive statement—like she had, but now she was going to have to substantiate it, and that wasn't funny.

'Well, don't look so scared,' Clifford said encouragingly. 'I'm not going out with a gun to shoot him. Who is it?'

'Er——' Amy searched her mind desperately, and one name emerged. She said it. 'Mike Saunders.'

Clifford looked positively startled. 'Mike Saunders?' He repeated. 'No! Mike Saunders from Bangalo Island? You're having me on, Amy. A man like *that* wants to marry you? That's a laugh—it really is! What's happened? You've met him over there and fallen in a heap at his feet—and you're trying to tell me it's serious? My dear girl, you must be imagining things!'

Curiously, Amy was hurt. Anyone would think she had nothing at all to recommend her, to hear him speak. Yet they had been engaged! She wasn't hideous, she wasn't brainless—she was only young. All the same, she wished she'd thought before she'd blurted out Mike Saunders' name. She should have made up a name, said Bill Smith—anything. Because of course Clifford had heard of Mike; most people up here had. And now she could hardly back down and pretend it was someone else with the same name, not when he knew she had been staying on Bangalo Island. She was in it up to her neck, and there was nothing for it but to go on. She drew a deep breath.

'You don't understand, Clifford. I—I went to school

with his sister. I met him years ago. I'm not imagining things.'

'Well, well!' He lit another cigarette and looked at her thoughtfully. 'You're certainly aiming high. I'd never have thought it of you. And here was I——' He coughed and started again. 'You won't be interested in the cane farm now—it's not worth a cracker compared to the Hotel Bangalo. It's a company, I suppose—a private company. And he'd own the bulk of the shares.'

'I wouldn't know,' Amy said shortly. She reached for her empty cup and looked at it uneasily.

'Then that's who flew you over to Cairns today, is it?' Clifford mused. 'And you want to be free—to break off our engagement.'

Amy nodded unhappily. That was what she wanted —because it was what he wanted, though he hadn't said so. She slid the ring off her finger and held it out to him. 'I'll have to give you this back.'

'No, keep it—keep it as a souvenir,' he said, looking at her curiously. 'You've really stunned me, Amy. I just don't know whether to believe you or not. Mike Saunders!'

Amy bit her lip. She thought she'd scream if he said that name again, and she glanced around uneasily, afraid some shopper having a coffee might hear the name and listen. Without thinking, she put the ring back on her finger and heard herself say in a low, tense voice, 'You'll have to believe me, Clifford.'

'I'm doing my best,' he said. 'But knowing you, I can't help suspecting you've been doing a bit of day-dreaming—plus a bit of the old limpet act.'

She felt the blood come into her cheeks and then recede. Was that a not very subtle reference to—to what she had felt for him, to how she had acted? Oh, Clifford, she thought, agonised. Is that how you saw me?

What a disaster it would have been to have married him and then found out what he really felt! Caught up in her crazy web of lies, she protested, 'I'm not day-dreaming!'

'He's actually asked you to marry him?'

She didn't even hesitate, she simply said, 'Yes,' and then hated herself for the lie. But surely Mike need never know. No one need ever know. She could go off back to Sydney, and that would be that. It didn't matter if Clifford did conclude, then, that she had been imagining things. He would be free, and he would think she wanted to be free too.

'What does your aunt think?' he asked then. 'Or haven't you told her yet?'

Amy shook her head 'I haven't told anyone.' Not even Mike, she thought wryly.

'Well, as I said before, you've amazed me. Come to think of it, I had the idea Mike Saunders' name was linked up with some artist or other who lives all by herself on one of the reef islands. But of course, if he's asked you to marry him—— You know, I think I'd like to meet him, Amy. You've really got me intrigued about this new heart-throb of yours. If you want to end our engagement, that's all right—but remember you'll be renouncing your share of your uncle's farm ... What time are you meeting Mike Saunders to go back?'

Amy's heart jumped. Clifford couldn't possibly come with her to meet Mike. She swallowed, then said quickly, 'I'm not meeting him. I'm flying with Bush Pilots. He's—staying with some people out of town to-night—it's a—a business matter.'

Clifford grimaced. 'Pity. But I suppose it can't be helped. Well, there's plenty of time yet for us to meet. But before we part, I've got to tell you something that's been on my mind.' He leaned towards her across the table, and she thought, 'Now he's going to tell me about Margaret Leslie.'

But he wasn't. It was something else.

'I'm selling the farm,' he said. 'I was feeling guilty about it because I hadn't discussed it with you and I didn't know what your feelings would be. That's why I wasn't keen on your coming north just now—I'm in the midst of negotiations. I'm planning to put the money into a business in Cairns.'

'Oh, what sort of a business?' Amy asked, a little taken aback.

'A shop—a boutique, as a matter of fact,' he said somewhat vaguely. 'I'm going into partnership with the present owner. We're going to extend, really make it something. Should be very profitable, with the tourist industry expanding as it has been doing.'

'I wish you luck,' Amy said uncertainly. She was sure it was Margaret Leslie's boutique he was talking about, but was *this* what Margaret had been urging him to tell her? Or did he have a more personal, intimate relationship with her? She couldn't ask, of course, and a moment later they both got up from the table and Clifford saw her into the street.

'Shall I come out to the airport with you?' he asked, not very enthusiastically.

'Oh no,' Amy protested hastily. 'You don't need to do that, Clifford.'

'All right—if you're sure you can manage on your own.'

'Quite sure,' she said, and felt a pang in her heart. They were talking to each other like a couple of polite acquaintances. How could it happen this way? Hadn't they ever been close—really close? Had she imagined it all?

She allowed him to put her into a taxi and they said goodbye.

'I'll be in touch,' Clifford said vaguely.

Amy glanced back as the taxi drove off, but he wasn't looking her way. His heart wasn't breaking, he was sceptical but quite definitely pleased by what she had told him. She was no longer sure what her own feelings were. She was confused, disturbed—hurt.

And as well, frantically worried by the lie she had told.

She leaned forward and told the taxi driver she had changed her mind about going to the airport. She wanted to go to the Civic Centre. And there, she thought, Mike Saunders would be waiting for her— and wouldn't he have a blue fit if he knew she'd said he'd asked her to marry him!

CHAPTER FIVE

AMY was over-talkative on the plane as they flew back to Bangalo. She exclaimed unnecessarily often about the various islands they flew over, and though she knew she sounded unnatural and nervy, she couldn't seem to help herself. She was terribly conscious of what she had told Clifford, and it was as if by rapid talk she could prevent Mike from finding out. Yet of course he need never know. She could leave Bangalo at any time she liked, and for Clifford's benefit she could invent an end to her relationship with Mike as easily as she had invented a beginning. Clifford wouldn't care; she knew that now. She was the one who had made the break, and that had freed him of any feeling of guilt.

'How are the wedding plans going?' Mike asked when she stopped talking to draw breath.

'Oh, all right. We—we've arranged—nothing definite,' she said flusteredly, then asked, 'What's that little island with the long spit of sand reaching out to the next one? I bet you could walk across that at low tide.'

'I reckon you could,' he agreed. 'But it's a reef, not sand . . . I take it you've followed my advice and not set a wedding date,' he resumed, not to be put off so easily.

'I haven't followed your advice,' she retorted perversely. 'We—we just agreed that we'd each—think about it. Besides, I have to consult Aunt Evelyn since she wants to give me my wedding.'

'Well, you've certainly got me baffled,' he remarked. 'I thought you'd rushed up here to get yourself married as fast as ever you could. I seem to recall you told me a *very* short time ago that marriage was the one and only thing that interested you.'

'Oh, you're twisting my words,' she said uncomfortably. 'Anyhow, what Clifford and I do is our own business. How did *your* day go? Did you find out from the Fiorenzas where Pauline is? That's where you went, isn't it?'

'Yes, I found out. I'll probably go to Italy in a week or so. I'm going to have a serious talk with Pauline and Sandro about their future. From what Mrs Fiorenza tells me of Sandro's interests, I think he might as well forget about going into business and concentrate on music and singing. If he can find himself some work, I'll agree to release some of Pauline's assets so he can take lessons. As for her, she'll have to learn to speak Italian if she's going to stay in Italy any length of time. But what happens remains to be seen.'

It sounded fair enough, Amy thought, and was thankful that after that Mike didn't return to the subject of her meeting with Clifford.

It was Karen who met them at the airstrip when they landed. She was anxious to hear Mike's news, and Amy, sitting in the back of the car, heard the story again.

'Oh that's great, Mike,' Karen enthused. 'That's a really clever idea—because he does have a fabulous voice. I do hope it all works out well for Pauli and that Sandro settles down and grows up.'

'It doesn't usually happen overnight,' he said grimly. 'Sandro's been spoilt—always had his own way. For all I know, he might resent my interference, but I'm going to see he doesn't get through Pauline's money and then vanish and that's that. She had no right to play around with him in the first place, and if I didn't think she was a good part to blame for encouraging him, I wouldn't lift a finger to help him.'

That, thought Amy, sounded more like Mike Saunders.

At Reception, she said a brief 'Thanks', then clambered out of the car and disappeared to her room to get ready for dinner.

She wore the black dress she had worn the night she dined with Mike, left her engagement ring on her finger, and was lucky enough to meet her American friends as she made her way to the restaurant. They asked her to join them for dinner, and they sat at a table for six. The other people were a honeymoon couple from Brisbane and a man of sixty or so whose name was Frank Milson. Bronzed, with keen blue eyes and white hair, he rather unexpectedly turned out to be an artist.

'I'm spending a painting holiday here,' he told them over dinner. 'Not for the first time either. I suppose you folks have walked up the mountain, had a look at the view and the rain forest?'

The honeymoon couple hadn't, the Americans, Pat and Ray, had, and a discussion of the various attractions of the island followed. Amy found it all very interesting, and it served to keep her mind off other things—such as Clifford, and what she had told him about herself and Mike.

After dinner the honeymoon couple vanished, and Amy went with the others into the lounge. There was to be a floor show that night, and the Americans were anxious to secure a table in a good position for watching it. Amy, who was not much in the mood for conversation, sat back in her chair and let the others talk, which they did quite animatedly as they all happened to be interested in the arts. When Frank insisted that she should have a drink, she produced her free voucher from her purse, which seemed to amuse him.

She was sipping the drink he had brought her when she saw a girl with long dark auburn hair come into the room. She wore a slightly faded sarong in a way that made you feel it was the kind of garment she always wore, and she went with great assurance to sit on a stool at the bar and order herself a drink. Amy was still looking at her with a mixture of admiration and curiosity when Frank exclaimed, 'That's Delona Ferguson, over at the bar. If you haven't heard of her, she's a local artist and a very good one. Shall I ask her to join us?'

'That would be super,' the Americans enthused, and Frank got up from his chair at once.

Amy had felt her heart go bump. So that was Delona Ferguson, the woman whose name she had heard twice now linked with that of Mike Saunders. Frank spoke to her and then she slipped off the stool and with her drink in her hand came across to join the small group. She was thin as a whip, Amy noticed, her face almost gaunt, her poise and self-assurance immense. But there was something about her that men would find fascinating. Amy didn't know what it was, but it was there—and she was certain it was something *she* didn't have, and never would. She could well imagine that Mike might be in love with her.

Frank introduced her all round and she sat down between him and Ray, relaxed and completely at ease.

'Delona lives on Nerina Island,' Frank remarked. 'In tropical simplicity—or splendour if you like. The kind of life one dreams about.'

'Alone?' Pat asked with a smile.

'Alone,' Delona said composedly, and sipped her drink. Over it she looked at Amy in a disconcertingly penetrating way, and then she looked at Ray.

'You have a boat, I guess,' said Ray, looking back at her admiringly.

'Good heavens, no! I don't need a boat. I only come across here once in three or four weeks, and that's just to keep in touch with the world—and maybe take a hot shower. I don't see a lot of people, I don't want to.'

'How do you get here?' Amy heard herself asking.

'Oh, someone comes for me. Paul Richards brought me across tonight—Mike couldn't make it. There he is, by the way——'

Amy followed her glance and felt a tremor run along her nerves. Mike, Karen and Paul had all come in, and they came straight across to where Amy was sitting. Because of Delona, of course. Amy smiled, but she felt tense and uncomfortable as extra chairs were moved up and they all sat down, Mike next to Delona now. The floor show was about to begin, and for that she was thankful. It was a singing and dancing act, but while part of her noted that it was extremely fast and professional, she didn't really pay much attention. She couldn't keep from thinking of what she had told Clifford—and she prayed that it would never reach the ears of anyone here. It was a dreadful thing to have done, to have said Mike had asked her to marry him when obviously he was wrapped up in Delona. What had Karen said?—that she was in line for a divorce—and presumably Mike was waiting for her.

When the floor show was over, he danced with her, and Amy rather reluctantly danced with Frank. After a couple of minutes he said, 'You're tired.' He stopped dancing and took her hand. 'Come and sit down and I'll get you a drink that will buck you up a bit. What've you been doing? Walking up the mountain?'

'No, I've been over to Cairns. I'm sorry about being so—so boring.'

'Good lord, you've got nothing to apologise about! I count myself fortunate to be able to enjoy the company of someone so young and so attractive. You're here on your own, I take it.'

'Yes.' She had tried to keep her engagement ring more or less out of sight all the evening, because she didn't want to have to talk about her non-existent fiancé. But she was afraid if she didn't wear it, Mike would catch her out—as he would have. She sat down again and waited with a sigh for Frank to bring her a drink, and at last he came back with something pink in a long frosty glass, with a swizzle stick and a straw.

'Is it raspberry syrup?' she asked suspiciously, and he laughed.

'I wouldn't insult you with anything so innocuous. It's got quite a kick—you try it.' He had brought a brandy for himself and as he sat down he raised his glass to her. 'Cheers!'

'Cheers,' Amy echoed. She tasted the drink and discovered it was quite definitely not raspberry syrup. She was going to have to be careful! But—oh heck, she was sick and tired of being careful, of being a head-mistress's niece. Recklessly she drank, and when Frank stared at her she told him, widening her eyes over the glass, 'I'm thirsty!'

He put a hand to his heart. 'My God, don't look at me like that! I'm too old for it! What are you doing here all by yourself, anyway, seeing you're engaged? Or do you just wear that ring for protection?'

Amy laughed, but she didn't answer, and to her relief he didn't press the point.

'It's a great place to come to, Bangalo,' he said. 'Swimming, tennis, snorkelling—Have you been out on the reef to see the coral?'

'Not yet,' she admitted, and let him talk about the reef and its beauties. Meanwhile, she watched Mike Saunders dancing with his girl-friend—in the same lazy easy way as he had danced with that other girl last night. She wondered if Delona would stay in his bungalow tonight—or if she would have a suite of her own, where Mike could visit her—if their relationship was 'that', she reminded herself cautiously.

She caught a few words of what Frank was saying— 'All this terrible business of the giant clam being en-dangered by the Taiwanese poaching on the reef. It's a pretty shocking affair. The human animal is respon-sible for an immense amount of destruction on this planet, but thank God we're beginning to have some sort of a conscience about it. I suppose you know the giant clam, Amy—the biggest bivalve shell in the world—can be over four feet across. I believe it plays an important part in the ecology of the reef, though I must admit I'm not well up on the scientific facts.'

'It's interesting,' said Amy with an effort at concen-trating on the subject. 'Everything in nature is so—so interlinked, isn't it? One of our teachers at school was always impressing on us the mess we're in danger of making in Australia with all our introduced plants and animals. Even bees.'

Encouraged by her interest, Frank mused on, and Amy's attention returned to Mike—dancing with that other girl, intent on her. Until unexpectedly he looked across the room at Amy just as he had last night. But this time she didn't look away, and neither did he, and she was aware of a sudden wild and illogical longing to be there with him, instead of Delona Ferguson. That devastating, lazy glance of his seemed to go straight to her heart so that every other thing was blotted out—Frank's voice, the dance music, the people on the floor. Then the mad moment was over and she thought dizzily, 'I'd better vanish—go to bed.' She stood up abruptly and discovered she really was dizzy. That drink—Frank looked at her in surprise and she realised she must have moved in the middle of something he was saying.

'I'm sorry, that drink was a real knock-out. I'm not all that used to alcohol. Will you excuse me?'

'Of course.'

In a minute flat she had escaped into the darkness. She felt absolutely dead tired all of a sudden, and she knew it wasn't just the alcohol. It was the sum total of her day—her meeting with Clifford, her own crazy fiction about Mike. It was knowing it was all over between her and Clifford—and it had something to do with the way she'd felt just now when she'd caught Mike's eye across the room. Probably guilt, she told herself firmly. Because if he ever knew what she had said he would be absolutely furious.

He was to know, as it happened. And very soon.

The next morning while she was at breakfast, Karen

came with the news that they were going over to Nerina Island with Delona.

'Wear something that doesn't matter,' Karen told Amy, 'and Mike says we must be at the jetty at ten o'clock sharp or we can't come. Delona's a work maniac. She has her whole day planned down to the last detail, though you'd never guess it.'

Amy wanted to go and yet she didn't want to go. She knew that if she said no, she would be sorry and wish she had gone. In fact, she was in a complete muddle. Back in her room, she put on a yellow skirt and a black and white top, thongs, a hat, and sun-glasses. And her ring. Oh yes, she must wear her ring, she thought bitterly. She must also decide when she was leaving the island. She'd have to go back to her headmistress aunt, she thought ironically, and she didn't really look forward to that. Aunt Evelyn had been wonderful to her, given her a home, taken a deep interest in everything she did—in a way, she had watched her like a hawk. While she hadn't wanted her to rush into marriage, she had been in favour of her marrying Clifford—because of the farm. It would mean she had something . . .

When Karen came to collect her, she was alone.

'We'll go ahead. Delona's yakking to that other artist—the one you were doing such a hot line with last night. And Mike's deep into something or other with Paul. Not me, I hope,' she added with a grin. 'I said we'd see them at the jetty.'

The sun was burningly hot as they walked round the beach to the jetty, and the water was blue-green and lazily innocent.

'Isn't it heavenly?' Karen murmured. 'I could stay here all my life—but not if I had to live like Delona.'

'What do you mean?' Amy asked. It sounded idle,

but she found she was acutely curious about Delona—Mike's girl-friend.

'Well, she has no electricity, no proper water supply. And her house—it's a shack—it's really primitive. She lives all alone, you know, and she doesn't encourage visitors. Only a few people, like Mike—and Steve. She has an old cowbell fixed to a post about fifty yards from the house and you're supposed to ring that to warn her you're coming. It's probably because she goes round naked most of the time. I've seen her in a tiny bikini and honestly, she's brown all over!'

They had reached the jetty by now where a small launch waited. It had an outboard motor, and there was an attractive fringed canopy for shade. The two girls went aboard and waited for quite a long time before Delona and Mike appeared. Mike was looking grim and unfriendly and offered no apology for keeping them waiting. He wore white shorts and no shirt, and Delona was in a wrap-around skirt and a faded T-shirt, her face completely without make-up. She must pander to Mike's tastes, Amy caught herself thinking, recalling his reaction to that luscious layer of lipstick she had worn in Cairns.

Mike stored away the two bulky straw bags he had been carrying and started up the motor, and soon Amy was enjoying the cool breeze as they skimmed across the glassy water. Nerina was only about fifteen or twenty minutes away and it was tiny. A sign on the white beach said NO LANDING PRIVATE PROPERTY KEEP OUT. Mike took the boat into shallow water, then climbed out and pulled it as far as he could on to the sand. Amy had to take hold of his hand as she jumped down from the boat, then she almost lost her balance in the soft swirling sand where the water dragged insistently, making it almost a quicksand. It was only his strength that held her up and her murmured thanks were greeted by a solid silence.

Her wet skirt clinging to her legs, she followed the other girls across the beach with its litter of broken coral and shells, and on to a sandy path shaded by coconut palms. Glancing back, she saw Mike securing the boat by jabbing the anchor into the sand, and soon he was following them with the bags. Amy saw the cowbell with its aggressive notice—Ring before proceeding, but of course no one took any notice of it. The house, when they reached it, was certainly a shack— a dilapidated building made of rough timber and palm leaves. Inside, it consisted of two rooms divided from each other by fine green mosquito netting. One room was bedroom and living room, the other, into which the door opened, was workroom and kitchen. The windows were unglazed and it was very hot and untidy, but very definitely an artist's house, with its stacks of paintings, and ethnic cloths covering chairs and an old divan.

Delona spent a few minutes unpacking footstuffs from the two straw bags, most of them going into a big kerosene refrigerator, and then she made coffee on a small gas burner. She didn't offer anything to eat, but passed round raw sugar in a pottery bowl and talked about the exhibition she was having early next year at the Hotel Bangalo.

'I want to hang the pictures myself, Mike. Is that asking too much? Will it be treading on anyone's toes?'

'Definitely not,' said Mike. He set down his coffee cup and Amy, sitting on a rickety chair—he and Delona were on the divan—thought he sounded preoccupied. And also that he seemed very much at home here.

'I'd like you to have a look at my ideas,' Delona said. 'Seeing there's going to be a business conference that first weekend, I thought I'd bash in as many big paintings as I could manage. If I possibly can, I'll stay here all summer and work—and pray this place doesn't get blown to pieces by a cyclone. Anyhow, if you've finished your coffee, I'd like to show you some sketches I've done.'

A moment later she and Mike went to the far end of the room, and Delona called back to Karen, 'If you're looking for a painting to give Amy, there are a few there on top of the little lacquer cabinet.'

Amy flinched. Karen had offered to give her one of Delona's paintings as a wedding present—and now there wasn't going to be a wedding. If she had any sense at all she'd tell Karen so, but somehow she couldn't, and rather wretchedly she went with Karen to look at the paintings. The little lacquer cabinet was a total wreck, but Delona was not in the least self-conscious about it. She was very natural and very like-able, Amy thought, despite her oddity. She tried to give her attention to the painting that Karen was holding up for her inspection, but she glanced through her lashes at Mike, looking through Delona's sketches with her at the far end of the room. Suddenly she caught his eye and looked away quickly. There was such a strange expression on his face as he looked at her—as if he were dissecting her. He had never looked at her that way before, and she wondered what he was thinking——

'Amy!' said Karen. 'Do you or don't you like this? I think it's tremendous.'

'I—I don't know,' Amy said helplessly. 'I don't think Clifford would——' Her voice trailed off, and Karen made a face.

'Okay, so Clifford has no taste. Then that's a great big shame. But I'm going to buy it all the same.' She raised her voice. 'Delona, I'd like this painting——'

Several minutes later, when Mike and Delona had finished their conversation and Karen had arranged to buy the painting, Mike said abruptly, 'We must be on our way. Karen has to get back to the office and I have things to see to. I'll be interested to see your final collection, Delona. I think it will really make headlines.'

She flashed him a brilliant smile. 'Before you go, you might as well take some fruit from the garden. I have so many passion-fruits I don't know what to do with them, and the pawpaws are falling off the trees.'

The garden—if it could be called that—was a wilderness. Flowers and vegetables and fruits rioted, and they soon had an enormous bag full of passion-fruits and pawpaws to take away with them. Delona said goodbye and went into her house—to proceed with her detailed plan of work for the day, Amy reflected—and the other three made their way back to the beach and the boat, Karen hugging the precious painting to her.

'Delona's a terrific person,' she remarked, as they started back across the water. 'It must be wonderful to be a dedicated artist—it must really give meaning to your life.'

'It could be compensation,' Mike said cryptically.

'How do you mean?' Karen demanded, but he didn't answer, he was too busy seeing them on to the boat. 'I was always hopeless at drawing,' she went on as she hopped agilely aboard and sat down. 'But you're artistic, Amy. You made some beaut pots at school in the craft class. Do you do any potting nowadays or are you too busy putting your creative energy into cooking, with Clifford in mind?'

Amy smiled rather palely, and Mike, starting up the motor, sent her such a cold look it made her blood curdle. He probably thought her terribly dull and uninteresting as well as being hopelessly immature, she thought resentfully.

That afternoon after lunch, she went back to her room to get into her swimsuit. She was going to lie on the beach and think the whole thing out, decide exactly what her future movements were to be. She had done no more than kick off her sandals when Mike came to her door.

'Are you there, Amy?' His voice sounded hard, and not particularly friendly.

'Yes.' Barefoot, heart thudding, she crossed to the insect screen and looked at him through it. 'What do you want?'

'To talk to you.' He slid the screen back as he spoke and stepped into the room. He wore white pants and an unbuttoned white jacket that showed he had no shirt underneath. His chest gleamed darkly against the whiteness and Amy felt dazzled. She watched him helplessly as he crossed to one of the cane armchairs and indicated the other. 'Sit down. I've got a few things to say to you.'

'About what?' she stammered. 'Do I—do you want me to leave? I was planning on going soon——'

'Shut up and listen,' he said abruptly. 'A phone call came through for you this morning, but you'd gone ahead to the jetty, so I took it.'

He paused and she moistened her top lip and tried to ignore the thoughts that had begun to seethe in her mind.

'Who—who was it?' she asked, and swallowed.

'Clifford North. He's flying over to Bangalo this evening and staying the night.'

Amy looked at him speechlessly, her dark eyes wide with fright. Clifford was coming! It couldn't be true!

She closed her eyes, feeling quite faint. When she opened them again Mike was looking at her grimly.

'He also told me the news,' he said, and waited for her reaction.

'What—what news?' she asked in a husky whisper, but of course she knew, and it was insupportable. It was a nightmare.

'Oh, come on now, Amy. You must know, since it was you who gave it to him in the first place. It appears that I want to marry you—or that you imagine I do. At all events, you're quite madly in love with me. Remember?' He smiled, and it wasn't pleasantly.

Amy wanted to die. She slumped back in her chair, her face dead white, and tried to think of something to say that would make it all come right. But there was nothing.

'I didn't mean you to know,' she said after what seemed an eternity. 'I'm sorry. I—I had to tell him something—it was the first thing that came into my mind.'

His eyebrows rose quizzically. 'But why? I thought you were happily engaged—looking forward to marrying.'

'Yes.' She said it flatly, despairingly. 'But I—I found out he doesn't really want to marry me. There's—someone else.'

'So you evened up the score by making up a story about your own love life?'

She shook her head bleakly. 'It wasn't like that. You see, he—he didn't tell me—he couldn't bring himself to hurt me. It was like you said, I guess.' She clasped her hands together and stared down at them unseeingly. 'He made a deathbed promise—to please my uncle and to—to please me. You said it could lead to disaster if we insisted on sticking to it, so I—pretended someone else wanted to marry me. It was easier for him that way,' she finished miserably.

'Your reasoning's crazy—and you're too soft,' he said. 'But why me, for pity's sake?'

She shook her head dazedly. 'I just couldn't think of anyone else offhand. I'm sorry—really I am.'

'You're sorry!' he repeated incredulously. 'Great heavens, you can do something as—as monstrous as that, and then say you're sorry and think it will be all right! It won't, you know. It's only as easy as that in a musical comedy or a fairy story. So what are you going to do about it?'

Amy looked at him in alarm. 'Please don't tell Clifford. Couldn't you just pretend it's true—just while he's here? Otherwise—well, I can't marry him when there's someone else and he'd feel so awful if it looked as though—well, as though he'd accepted my uncle's farm and then—then kicked me out.'

'And hasn't he done that?'

'No,' she said instantly. 'I'm the one who broke it off. After all, it's—it's not his fault he's fallen in love with someone else, is it? But he's so—honest he wouldn't back out of it. Don't you see?'

'I see plenty,' Mike said dryly. 'And you had to sacrifice yourself on the altar of love, didn't you, Amy? Very noble of you—and you dragged me into it whether I like it or not. Well, I don't agree with your principles, but if you insist I suppose I'll back up your story. You do insist, do you? You're quite sure of that?'

It was a curious way to put it to her, but—'Yes,' she said, and added rather tardily, 'Please,' and wished with all her heart she hadn't got herself into this more than embarrassing situation.

'That ring,' he said. He had got to his feet and he stood looking down at her, his eyes hard. 'Why didn't you give it back? Couldn't you bring yourself to part with it?'

'Clifford wouldn't take it. He wanted me to keep it as a souvenir.'

'Very generous,' he commented, his mouth twisting. 'Well, souvenir or not, you're going to take it off right now, and you'll never wear it again.'

Amy's eyes widened. The menacing look in his eyes alarmed her and she slipped the ring quickly from her finger and closed her fingers over it. Suddenly she was appalled at what lay ahead of her. She thought of Karen—of Paul—of Delona Ferguson. Of everyone at the hotel with whom Mike was associated.

'I—I wish you'd stopped Clifford from coming,' she faltered. 'I would have.'

'And I could have,' he agreed. 'By rubbishing the whole thing. However, I was intrigued to hear you believed I had such—honest intentions towards you.'

'What do you mean?'

'Well, you and I both know I've been playing you along a bit, that I've made a few passes at you. What I didn't realise was that I'd qualified as an ardent suitor —or that you were so desperately in love with me.'

She bit her lip. 'I'm not—I've explained that. And we don't need to let anyone know—Karen or—or Delona—or——'

Mike's eyebrows peaked. 'No? I don't honestly think we're going to convince Clifford if we three seal ourselves in a sort of plastic bubble and perform our little drama there, with no audience. I'm afraid you're going to have to take the full consequences of your impulse, Amy. That's if you're determined to protect Clifford's tender feelings. Frankly, if it were left to me, I'd tell him he's a miserable bastard using shady practices to get hold of a property that obviously should have been yours—and now not even having the guts to tell you he's teamed up with another woman.'

'That's not fair!' she exclaimed angrily. 'He didn't tell me because—because he knew how I felt about him. He'd have kept his promise.'

'I doubt it,' he said sceptically. 'He's hardly been rushing you off your feet, has he? At all events, if we're going ahead with this, then we're going to do it my way, and we're not hushing it up. For a start, you can pack up your junk and I'll have one of the housemaids come and get this room ready for Clifford. It's no use protesting, we don't have another vacant suite. I'll give you half an hour to get ready and then I'll come and escort you personally to my own bungalow.'

'You—you needn't carry it as far as that,' she stammered, bewildered at the way things were turning out.

'Believe me, we'll be carrying it a great deal further,' he said, his mouth twisting. 'You're playing in the big league now, Amy, and the game's likely to be rough.' He tilted his head back slightly in a gesture of command. 'Come here.'

'Why?' she breathed out. He didn't answer and after a moment she got up from her chair but didn't move in his direction. 'What do you want?' she quavered.

'Come here,' he repeated.

'I—I won't,' she faltered, knowing well enough he meant to kiss her.

'You really want it all your own way, don't you?' he gritted. 'Look, I'm doing you a big favour, Amy, and if I say come, you'll come. Otherwise I'll do as I said and tell your friend Clifford a few home truths that he definitely won't like.'

Ten seconds passed and then stiffly, unwillingly, conscious of the indignity of her bare feet, Amy went to him. He put his hands on her shoulders and looked down into her eyes and she looked back—and remembered with a shock the way she had felt last night watching him on the dance floor with Delona.

'Will you marry me, Amy?' he said.

Her head jerked up and her eyes widened in surprise. 'What do you mean?'

He narrowed his eyes. 'You know what I mean. You've already told Clifford I've asked you that question. Now it's true. The next thing is for you to say yes. So let's hear it.'

'Yes,' she said unwillingly.

'Great. And then I kiss you,' he said. 'Like this.'

She remembered as his lips met hers that he'd told her to relax her mouth, but she didn't. It was a ridiculous charade they were acting out, and she supposed he regarded it as payment for what he was doing for her.

'That's not kissing,' he said, after a moment. 'A girl who knows as little as that about kissing has no business saying yes to any man. It might have passed fifty years ago, but not today. Come on now, loosen up. Remember you're a woman and I'm a man. I've asked you to marry me and I want you. I want the right to lie with you at night—or in the daytime, come to that; to make love to you, to share my dreams and my work with you, to make you happy—to make you my life, in fact. I want the pleasure your body can give me, and I want to give you pleasure too. If you stiffen up like that, I might as well embrace a wooden doll.'

He reached for her lips again and she turned her head aside quickly. 'We—we don't have to do all this. I—I can't,' she murmured, somehow shocked by the things he had said. Clifford had never talked to her that way—she'd never imagined a man saying such things to her——

'You can't? How about if you pretend I'm Clifford, then?' He took hold of her jaw roughly and forced her face back to his, but instead of kissing her he looked steadily into her eyes and said softly, 'Do you know you have very beautiful eyes, Amy Martin? And your mouth—it leaves nothing to be desired.' He let go her chin and traced the outline of her upper lip with one finger so gently that it tickled excruciatingly.

'You said it—it tasted of raspberry syrup,' she protested huskily. He had stopped stroking her upper lip and she ran her tongue over it exploringly, discovering it still felt sensitive. Some of the tension had gone out of her and she had a sudden mad desire to laugh—or to cry.

'That was another day,' he said lightly. He slid his hand under her shirt and caressed her bare skin, then brushed his fingers lightly up over her rib cage till they stopped at the swell of her breast. She stood still even though she felt alarmed and her breath quickened. No one had ever done that to her before. Of course she knew it was done—that and much more. But that it should be Mike Saunders teaching her, when she'd never loved any man but Clifford—When his mouth moved to cover hers, she closed her eyes and stayed passive as his lips explored her own, warm, persuasive, sensuous. She was aware of a sort of rising curiosity, an odd sensation of expectancy, but she refused to give in to it, and finally Mike let her go and said dryly, 'I'm not Clifford. Well, that's too bad for you, isn't it, Amy?'

She didn't meet his eyes and she felt the colour come into her face as she said in a low voice, 'I'd better pack.'

'You do that,' he agreed. 'It's a nice safe occupation, isn't it?'

CHAPTER SIX

LATER, when Mike had escorted her to the bungalow and left her there, Amy discovered he had already told Karen about their 'engagement'. Karen was there to greet her and to exclaim, 'Isn't it fantastic—romantic?' And Amy felt stunned that she could accept it and believe it so easily. But that was probably because her opinion of her brother was pretty high.

'We're having a celebration dinner tonight—champagne—mud-crabs——' She rolled her eyes expressively. 'Paul's arranged it all—Mike told him this morning before we went over to Nerina.' She had gone into the bedroom Amy was to have and flung herself on to the bed while Amy unpacked in a complete daze. So Mike had arranged the celebration this morning—he had decided long before he talked to her about it that they would go ahead with her pretence. She couldn't understand him. In fact she had the weird sensation that she was dreaming—that Clifford wasn't coming at all and that no one knew about the lie she had told.

'I'll bet Clifford's *wild*,' Karen said. 'But it serves him right, neglecting you as he did. If he hadn't let himself be bluffed by Dainie's ideas on morality you and Mike wouldn't have had a chance to fall in love. But I'm glad you did—I always thought he was wasting his life on Delona.' She sat up and put a hand over her mouth. 'I'm being tactless! But I really don't think you should worry about Delona, Amy—it's just one of those things men get themselves into, and her painting means more to her than anything else ... I suppose you

106

told Clifford when you met him in Cairns—you'd want him to be the first to know.'

'Yes,' Amy agreed, her back to Karen as she shook out some of the things she had bundled carelessly into her suitcase. Oh dear, yes—Clifford had certainly been the first to know—he'd known even before Mike!

'I'm sure you and Mike will be happy, Amy,' Karen said after a moment. 'I really think it's terrific. I should have suspected something when Mike was so disagreeable—he knew you were engaged and I suppose he thought he couldn't have you.'

Amy listened and didn't disillusion her.

She wore a silky white dress with a crossover top for the dinner, and she didn't see Clifford until then. A table for eight had been laid at one end of the restaurant, and the engagement party consisted of Karen and Paul, Coral Hailey the hostess, Peter Grey, the guest relations officer, June who ran Reception, Mike, herself, and of course Clifford. The chef himself came in, the meal was very splendid, and there was champagne at every table. To Amy's relief, no public announcement was made. However, the news spread rapidly around the restaurant that Mike Saunders was engaged, and a constant stream of people came to the table to offer their congratulations—to kiss Mike if they were female, to kiss Amy if they were male. Various guests, Con, the dance band leader, Steve from the hotel launch, Harry who ran the bar, the waitresses, the drink waiters—everyone was interested, everyone came. Amy's cheeks were flushed, the champagne had gone to her head, and in a crazy way she was almost deceived herself.

Clifford was certainly convinced.

Seated near her, he murmured over the dessert—a spectacular Bombe Alaska—'I'm beginning to realise to the full why you abandoned me and the cane farm in such a hurry, Amy. You're doing very well for yourself, aren't you?'

Amy nodded. Of course, if it were all true she *would* be doing very well. But——

Afterwards they all went into the lounge where Con and the dance band launched immediately into some romantic music, and everybody clapped when Mike took her on to the floor to dance. Her heart beat fast and she had the feeling her legs were about to give way, and she thanked heaven he danced the way he did. Not holding her close, the minimum of movement, but he looked down into her face all the time with that same laconic, quizzical expression she had seen him wearing when he danced with other girls. Only—only it seemed to her there was something else, something unreadable, at the back of his eyes as she gazed into them as if transfixed.

When he took her back to the others, Clifford asked her to dance, and the minute they were on the floor he said aggrievedly, 'I suppose you realise I've been pretty rocked by this whole performance, Amy. I thought you'd dreamed it all up—that's why I wouldn't take my ring back.'

'Was it?' She stared at him in surprise. 'But, Clifford, I thought——' She stopped. She couldn't mention Margaret Leslie, and she finished awkwardly, 'I thought you said if I met someone else you'd let me go.'

'Yes, but I hardly thought you had it all lined up and would rush off to the arms of another man the minute the words were out of my mouth. Particularly after all that trauma when your uncle was dying and I promised I'd marry you.'

Amy sighed helplessly. Now *she* was beginning to

feel guilty, and she said in bewilderment, 'Then I'm—I'm sorry, Clifford.'

'All right, you're sorry. But if Mike Saunders throws *you* over, and he could, you're scarcely his type, then don't imagine you can come running back to me, that's all.'

'No, I won't,' she said dryly, thinking of Margaret. She felt curiously remote from Clifford. The love between them—if it ever had been love—seemed to be well and truly dead.

Presently she said, 'You were telling me about selling the farm, Clifford—going into a business partnership in Cairns. Who is it with?'

'What interest is that to you?' he said. 'We're finished.'

It was like a slap in the face, and after that they were both silent. Amy had meant so well, she had meant to save him from embarrassment and guilt, and now he had somehow turned the tables on her so *she* was the guilty one. She bit her lip, unable to keep back a few tears, and it was at that minute that Mike interrupted them.

'I suggest we go over to my bungalow for a few minutes,' he said. 'You'd probably like to know what plans Amy and I have made, seeing you've been—er—involved with my fiancée for some time.' As he finished speaking he looked at Amy and saw the tears on her lashes, and she supposed he would think they were for Clifford. She wondered anxiously what he was going to tell Clifford about their plans, and wished he would keep it to himself instead of going on and on, making things more and more complicated so that it was going to be difficult to extricate themselves from the situation.

However, Clifford evidently wanted to hear their

plans, and they all walked over to the bungalow.

When they reached the quarry-tiled terrace that looked on to the beach, Mike told her, 'Go and get some fruit punch from the fridge, Amy, and bring a few glasses.'

She hurried to obey and as soon as she was inside the house she wished she hadn't. She shouldn't have left those two alone. She didn't trust Mike and she didn't want Clifford being accused of dishonesty. It didn't matter about the cane farm—she could earn her own living. In her haste to get back to the terrace quickly, she broke one of the glasses and had to clear up the pieces, and she was feeling thoroughly demoralised and very anxious by the time she rejoined the men.

'What's up, Amy?' Mike asked mockingly as she put the tray down shakily on the table and the glasses rattled together. 'Did you think your ex-fiancé and I might have come to blows?'

Your ex-fiancé! That was the first reference he had made in Clifford's presence to the relationship that had existed between him and Amy—but of course he could hardly pretend he didn't know about it.

'Sit down, for God's sake,' snapped Mike. 'By the sound you made crashing about in the house you're hardly to be trusted to pour the drinks.' He poured them himself, and Clifford drank thirstily. Amy could see in the soft light from the ground-level lamps that he was perspiring.

'I've just been remarking,' Mike said then, 'that I didn't expect a cane farmer to be civilised. If I'd been in Clifford's position I know damned well I'd have been violent if someone had taken my girl from me so unscrupulously. Especially a girl like Amy Martin,' he concluded—quite unnecessarily, she thought, feeling herself flush deeply.

Clifford scowled. 'All I want is for Amy to be happy. And if you want my honest opinion, I think she could be making a mistake. You're a lot too old for her.'

'You think so?' Mike said pleasantly. 'I disagree. If there's any problem, it's that Amy's too young—and I don't mean in years. But that can be remedied, and as from now she's going to grow up fast. We plan to be married as soon as I can make the arrangements— in no more than a week's time, and quite probably less.'

Amy almost fell over. In a week or less they were getting married! That was really going too far, and it was almost more than she could do not to burst out and tell Mike so.

Clifford uttered a short laugh. 'I'm afraid you'll have Amy's aunt to contend with. She'll want Amy to be married in Sydney, and I can tell you she won't like the look of all this hurry.'

Mike raised his eyebrows and looked amused. 'I'll make my plans to suit myself. But I don't expect to have any trouble with Miss Dain. I'm sure she'll see my point of view when she knows about our engagement. I'll be going to Italy shortly, and I'm certainly not leaving Amy behind. I want her to come with me—as my wife.' He glanced at Amy as he spoke and she glared back at him angrily. 'The wedding will be in Cairns, and I hope you'll be able to spare the time to come along. I understand you're extraordinarily busy these days——'

'I'll come,' Clifford muttered, and Amy felt furious with Mike for his contemptuous manner.

'Good.' Mike got to his feet, indicating that the conversation was over—his plans had been revealed, he was finished with Clifford. 'I've arranged for you to see something of the island in the morning. Your plane leaves at one-thirty, by the way. Goodnight. I hope you sleep well.'

Clifford said goodnight, managed a smile for Amy, and walked away. She felt bad about him and very confused. She didn't know what she had expected of him, but she felt he had somehow shown up in a bad light, and she was vaguely unhappy. It was all Mike's fault. He'd been overbearing—rude. As for his plans——

As soon as Clifford was out of earshot she burst out, 'You're paying me out, aren't you? Rubbing my nose in my—my lie!'

She stood on the terrace facing him, and he folded his arms across his chest and looked back at her impassively.

'What the hell are you complaining about?'

'You know perfectly well! Telling Clifford all those lies about being married and—and going to Italy. Putting on that publicity stunt to begin with, letting everyone in the hotel know—believe—we're engaged. When it was only Clifford who needed to be told——'

'I'm afraid I don't see it that way. We're either engaged or we're not—in other words, you can't eat your cake and have it, Amy. I agreed to back your story up. Under the circumstances.'

'What circumstances?' she demanded suspiciously.

'Oh, come on now—to deny the truth of what you'd said would have made you a liar, and I couldn't do that to a nice little female who's a friend of my sister. And quite apart from that, you surely must be aware of your—considerable physical attractions.'

'My physical attractions!' she gasped, reddening. 'What—what has that to do with it?'

Mike smiled cynically. 'Are you really asking me that? Don't you know even the first thing about sex appeal? You happen to have a whole load of it and I for one am very strongly aware of it—even if Clifford isn't. Or wasn't. It may be regrettable since you're so damnably immature, but as I intimated to your friend Clifford, I'll be working on that. And isn't your own self-avowed aim in life to get married? ... Come on, we're going inside.'

He reached out a hand and she stepped back, feeling the blood go from her face. He had said he was going to work on her immaturity, and the thought made her quail.

'I'm waiting here till Karen comes back,' she said quaveringly.

'Little coward,' he mocked. What do you think I plan to do with you? And don't you want to know what love's all about?'

Love? 'No,' she said, moistening her upper lip.

'Well, if you're not coming inside, shall we take a swim? Karen could be another hour or two yet.'

'I—I don't know.' She glanced at the glinting waters beyond the palms. If she said no to that as well, then what other alternative was there? And exactly what had Mike meant by 'coming inside'? She wished Karen would come back. It was too unnerving being alone with Mike.

'Make up your mind,' he said impatiently, and she was aware of his glance travelling down the length of her body and back again.

'Well—all right,' she agreed. 'I—I am hot.'

'So am I,' he said. 'Damned hot ... Swimsuits?'

'What do you mean?'

'I'm asking you if you want to wear a swimsuit or if you'd rather bathe in the nude.'

Amy nearly died of horror. 'Of course I don't want to bathe in the nude!' she exclaimed indignantly. She began to move indoors, then turned back to ask in a choked voice, 'You're not, are you?'

'Not what?' he asked, amused, and when she said nothing he mocked, 'Can't you even bring yourself to say it? You do have a lot to learn—you must be a mass of inhibitions ... All right, I won't swim in the nude if you'd rather I didn't. I don't want to shock you. I suppose you've never seen a naked male in your life.'

Amy hadn't, but she wasn't going to say so. She went inside to her room, shut the door, and got into her swimsuit as fast as ever she could. She hadn't put the light on, and through the curtains she could see Mike on the terrace, so she knew exactly where he was. The yellow maillot with its plunging neckline seemed too daring to her now, and after a moment's thought she found a pearl brooch that Aunt Evelyn had given her and pulling the edges of the neckline together, pinned them firmly. That was—safer, she thought. It made her feel less vulnerable.

She went outside and told him jerkily, 'You can change now.'

He looked her over swiftly and noticed the pearl brooch instantly, and his sensual mouth twisted in a smile of contempt. 'You silly little fool—don't you know you're only drawing attention to your breasts, doing that?'

Amy flinched at his remark, her hand going defensively to her breast. In a couple of strides he was beside her and had pulled her savagely into his arms— and she remembered him saying she was in the big league now and the game might be rough.

'Let me go!' she gasped, struggling against him, but Mike took no notice of her. Holding her to him, he ran the fingers of one hand through her hair from the nape of her neck, twisting it so that it hurt when she pulled her head back. The other hand was on her bare waistline. She was sticky with perspiration and her breath was coming fast.

'Don't—don't do that!' she panted as his face came nearer to hers. 'Karen will see us—Paul——'

'Who cares?' His voice was low and rough. 'This sort of thing is only to be expected of people who are going to be married.'

'But we're not,' she protested. 'You know it was only so Clifford would feel in honour bound to——'

'I don't give a damn about Clifford,' he ground out. 'I dislike the bastard—I'm doing nothing as a favour to him. We're engaged and everybody knows it. And don't tell me you didn't say yes when I asked you,' he concluded, moving his hand against her waist.

'It was only because you insisted—you made me,' she breathed.

'And I'm still insisting—I'm still going to make you. Do you think I'm going to let you announce to everyone the moment Clifford's gone that we've been playing some silly game?'

'No, of course not, and I—I wouldn't——' It was ridiculous, talking to him like this, their faces only inches apart, his fingers tangled in her hair, while he drew her more and more closely against his body. 'But when you go to Italy, I'll go back to Sydney, and it will all just——' Her voice faded into nothing.

'Be forgotten?' he suggested. 'I'm afraid it won't . . . Are you by any chance hoping you'll have made Clifford so jealous he'll want to marry you after all?'

'No,' she said wretchedly.

'What was he saying when you were dancing with him? That he was jealous—that he wanted you back?'

Amy swallowed. Clifford hadn't said he was jealous. He'd been sceptical of her romance—he'd said she wouldn't be able to come back even if she wanted to. 'He said——' she began, not really knowing what she was going to tell him, but Mike let her get no further.

'Shut up,' he said hoarsely. 'I don't want to know.'

His mouth covered her own and she had another lesson in love—or was it sex?—and not as elementary as he had given her in the afternoon. He didn't tell her that he wanted her this time, but she knew it. She learned it in a way she had never experienced before. She felt the urgency rising in his body and didn't know whether to ignore it or to struggle—to break away from him. But with his mouth over hers, with the way he was holding her, she had no choice. All she could do was to stay passive, unresponsive, and wait for him to let her go.

When he did so, it was to say with a groan, 'Oh God, you don't know a single thing, do you, Amy? You're hopelessly innocent, damn you. Go on down to the beach, I'll join you in a minute.'

She walked down to the sand and stood there feeling it cool under her bare feet. She was disturbed about herself, about her total innocence. 'Damn you,' Mike had said, and that had hurt. Yet why should she care? He didn't mean a thing to her. She'd been mad to get herself involved with him this way, but she wasn't going to marry him—even though he said he was still insisting. Oh, if only he hadn't made such a public performance of their so-called engagement! Why had he? She could only hope that her innocence might be her salvation, that he'd give her up as a bad bet. That was what Clifford was expecting.

Clifford. Staring at the dark sea, she thought of him, here on this island, so close. She wished he had told her about Margaret Leslie; she would have had more respect for him if he had. She wondered if they planned to marry or if their relationship would be a casual one, like the one Margaret had had with the man who had lived with her before. 'I'd have married him,' she thought. 'We'd have had children—I'd have looked after him.'

'Really?' she asked herself. Because suddenly it was impossible to imagine being Clifford's wife—sharing a home with him, waiting for him in the evenings——But perhaps that was because she could no longer put it against the setting of the cane farm. That was to be sold. The old familiar background was vanishing along with a lot of other things.

She heard a movement and turned to find Mike had joined her.

'Are you coming in?' he asked briefly, and strode past her without waiting for her to answer. He looked darkly masculine in his black trunks as he waded into the water, submerged, and then began swimming. Amy watched, but she didn't follow him. Away out, the dark shapes of islands loomed like shadows, and a few lights glimmered. The hotel lights were hidden behind the little rocky headland, so that she and Mike seemed cut off from the rest of the world. She thought of Delona on her tiny island. Was she too wrapped up in her art to satisfy Mike—to want to be his wife, once she had her divorce? For the life of her, she couldn't see it. No, she thought, Mike wasn't really going to marry Amy Martin. He was doing what she had said—teaching her a lesson. And she was finding it unexpectedly painful.

She had walked as far as the edge of the water, but she couldn't make herself go in, follow Mike. If he really wanted her to go in with him, then he would come back for her.

He didn't. As far as she knew, he didn't even glance shorewards, but when he had had enough he came wading out, water dripping from him as he ran his hands over his wet head.

He made no comment on the fact that she hadn't gone into the water. He merely asked, 'Are you coming inside now? The lights are on—Karen's back.'

He kept walking while he spoke, and Amy followed him, her head down. For some reason she wanted to cry.

She didn't go out with Clifford next day to see around the island. She wasn't invited, and in fact she didn't even see him before he went, as she had breakfast with Karen in Mike's bungalow.

'Mike was up at the crack of dawn,' Karen remarked as they ate fresh pawpaw and drank coffee together on the terrace. 'He went out in the boat.'

'With Clifford?' Amy asked.

Karen laughed. 'Don't look so worried, Amy. What are you imagining? That Clifford will knock him overboard and drown him, or something like that? Mike can look after himself—and Clifford didn't show any signs of violence last night, did he? In fact, I thought he took it all rather too well. In my opinion, any girl in her senses would prefer Mike to him. I suppose that sounds a bit rude, but it's a fact. I hope you're glad you waited, anyhow, otherwise you and Mike would never have met—or not until it was too late,' she amended.

Amy, listening to her babble on, suddenly suspected she was talking fast to hide something, and thought she could guess what it was : Mike had taken his boat over to Nerina to visit Delona. That must be it. But while Karen probably imagined he wanted to tell her the news before anyone else did, Amy thought he would be telling her the truth of the matter—which was that he didn't really intend to marry her, Amy, at all.

After breakfast Karen went off to the office, and Amy looked for Clifford. Not because she really wanted to see him, but because she thought it was the right thing to do. He wasn't in the lodge, and one of the house-maids, seeing her there, told her he had gone out with a crowd of other guests on a walk up the mountain, under the leadership of Coral Hailey.

Amy went back to the bungalow. Everything had been cleared up and tidied in her absence, and after a while she got into her swimsuit—she had removed the ridiculous brooch from it last night—and having smoothed on plenty of sun-block, she put on a hat and sun-glasses and went to lie in the shade of the palms. It was time to do some thinking.

The sea was as pale and clear and green as chryso-prase, and the sand was dazzlingly white. Waves broke lazily on the fringing reef some way out, and she lay back languorously in the fibreglass lounger and tried to concentrate on working out a sensible plan of campaign. One moment she wondered if she should pack—leave on the plane with Clifford this afternoon, if there was a spare seat. But that presented difficulties—Clifford would be suspicious, and moreover, where did she go from Cairns? She had to think that out too. Anyhow, she had an idea that Mike wouldn't let her slip through his fingers as easily as that. He hadn't nearly finished teaching her a lesson yet. Quite probably she was worrying over nothing. When he *had* finished with her, he would send her off without a qualm—but strictly in his own time. Back to her headmistress aunt, a little more grown up, a little less innocent—or maybe a lot less so——

A shadow fell beside her on the white crystalline sand, and she looked up. It was Mike, shirtless, brown-limbed, wearing white shorts.

'What are you thinking about, Amy?'

'Leaving here,' she said promptly, and coloured, suddenly aware that she was lying flat on her back on the lounger in a very abandoned way. And of the fact that his eyes were lingering on her full breasts, only just decently covered by the yellow swimsuit.

He said abstractedly, 'Such a ripe figure—such a green girl . . . So what were your thoughts on leaving?'

'I was wondering how soon I can leave,' she said huskily, sitting up so that the brim of her white hat completely hid her face from him, and discovering that now, all she could see of him was from just above his navel down, which was rather distracting.

'You'll leave on the day we go to Cairns together—for our wedding,' he said coolly. 'That's how soon you can leave, Amy. No girl walks out on me when I've been seen running around her in circles.'

'Don't be—silly,' she faltered. 'I know you're just teaching me a lesson. If you want to save your—your pride, or something, then I'll stay till you go to Italy, I suppose. But only till then. You can stay away till it's all blown over, can't you? And then I don't care what you tell Karen—anyone. That you got sick of me, that I'm too immature for you—anything. I am, anyhow, aren't I?'

'Sure you are,' he said with maddening cynicism. 'But immaturity doesn't stop anyone buying a puppy and training it. One thing is certain, you'll grow up. You've got a woman's body, and someone's going to teach you all about life pretty soon—particularly now you've rid yourself of one of your childhood delusions.'

'Well, *you're* not going to teach me,' she interjected.

'Why not?' He moved and sat down on the end of the lounger so he could see her face again. 'I'd have thought I was right at the head of the queue.'

'What about Delona?' she burst out, embarrassed. 'She's getting divorced, isn't she?'

'Who the hell's been talking to you about Delona?' he demanded explosively.

She didn't answer. She said, 'Isn't that where you went in your boat this morning—to see her—to tell her——'

One corner of his mouth curved upward. 'I believe you're jealous, Amy. Now that's really a good sign— much more healthy than your protective attitude to Clifford.'

'I'm not jealous,' she interjected, but he swept on.

'Yes, I went to see Delona, and yes, I told her.'

'What did you tell her?'

'That I'm being married. What did you think?'

She drew a deep breath. 'As a matter of fact, I don't believe you. I think you told her that you're going to break it off, that you've just been making me pay for using you the way I did.'

His brows rose. 'You have been doing some creative thinking,' he marvelled. 'But you don't know me very well if you think I'd go to quite some trouble to build what's no more than a house of cards. I'm not that kind of man, I assure you. When I say I'll do a thing, I damned well do it.'

Amy looked at him warily. She still didn't think he meant to marry her, a girl so ignorant of sex and love, so—so green——

'But why?' she faltered. 'I mean, why would you marry me?'

'Why?' Mike got up from the lounger and stood looking down at her, his grey eyes enigmatic. 'Well, let's see—— Because of your sexy looks—and your virginity. And because'—he screwed up his eyes and his mouth curved slightly—'because I imagine I can see into the future. How will that do? And to prove to you that I'm serious, I've been working out our plans. The reception will be at the best hotel in Cairns. Unfortunately I can't arrange to have it here at such short notice—we have too many bookings. I'll send a cable to your aunt, and I'll fly over to Cairns this afternoon to see about a marriage licence and to make numerous other arrangements. You're staying here. You can make a list of people you want to invite, and we'll cable out the invitations once the date is fixed.'

'But—but my dress,' Amy heard herself stammering, even while her head swam with the craziness of it all. 'It's not finished—I——'

'Your dress?' His voice expressed incredulous amusement. 'Your *wedding* dress? Are you for God's sake talking about some gown you intended to wear when you married Clifford? You surely can't contemplate wearing that when you marry me?'

'Oh.' Amy leaned back again and closed her eyes and felt tears squeeze their way between her lids and run hotly down her cheeks. She couldn't understand why she was beginning to weaken, to give in. Was it simply because it seemed useless to protest, to fight? Or had she somewhere along the line begun to exchange a girlish dream for another, freakish, one? If so—how had it happened, and when? She couldn't possibly be falling in love with Mike. Quite definitely not ... As for the dress, he was right, of course. She couldn't wear it. Though not because it would remind her of Clifford. Rather because it wasn't the sort of dress one would wear when one married someone like Mike Saunders. Correction—*If* one married someone like Mike Saunders. And illogically, she was going to do just that. Beating him at his own game? she wondered. Because he was certainly a good catch—Clifford had been aware of that.

She opened her eyes and looked straight at him, and he leaned down and removed her sun-glasses and saw her tears.

'You soppy little girl! Why don't you grow up? Forget your childish affair with Clifford North. I'll take you to Cairns and you can buy yourself some new wedding finery with me in mind. It's time to face up to the facts of life. You'll be saying farewell to Clifford for ever in less than two hours' time. You can have lunch with him in the restaurant and then you can wave him off in the hotel car and forget him. This afternoon you can occupy yourself making out that list; I'll want it when I come back this evening ... Now go inside and get dressed, and you'd better be quick about it.'

Amy went.

And after that, it all happened as he had planned, more or less. She lunched with Clifford, and they were very stiff with each other. She went along to the airstrip with him in the hotel car and saw the little Bush-Pilots plane take off with him in it, and then, with a feeling of relief, she walked back to the hotel complex and completely forgot Clifford. Who would ever have thought it could happen?

She sat out on the terrace in front of the bungalow and made a list of people she wanted to invite to her wedding. It was a very small list. It was a lot to ask of people to fly up to Cairns from Sydney. There was Aunt Evelyn, of course, and a couple of the younger teachers she had been friendly with—though they wouldn't be able to get away because it was term time. If Aunt Evelyn approved, she would come, of course. Amy wondered what she would think about her apparent change of heart—what she would think about her niece marrying Mike Saunders of Bangalo Island. She just wouldn't believe it!

Amy wrote down Clifford's name, and the Delucas', and after a moment she wrote down Margaret Leslie. Then she crossed it out. It might upset Clifford if he thought she knew about Margaret.

After that there were only a few old school friends, and she couldn't really see any point in having Mike cable them. She didn't want a big reception under the circumstances, even if it was to be held at the best hotel in Cairns and no expense spared.

When she had made the list, she thought about her wedding dress. She'd spend a lot on it. She'd get something really good, something that would knock Mike's eye out. The dress she had been making for her marriage to Clifford had been white—long, immaculate, demure, high-necked and long-sleeved. So she would buy something completely different from that. Would it be a church wedding? She hadn't even asked Mike. She didn't even know what he felt about God. For herself, she believed in God—quite simply, because if you were completely materialistic then you weren't really intelligent. Life was so mysterious. And so, she found herself thinking, was love.

She went into the bungalow and wandered from room to room and decided she liked it. It was going to be her home. That was strange. And yet it had good vibes, as far as she was concerned. So didn't that mean something? Didn't it mean that, somehow, there was a chance for her and Mike to make a good life together?

She finished up in her own bedroom in front of the mirror. A dark-haired, dark-eyed girl in a white skirt and a green top—a boob tube, that was what it had been called in the shop where she'd bought it. She smiled wryly at the crudity of the name.

Well, she was going to wear white when she married Mike. Simple white, elegant white.

She had stopped fighting it, in fact. It was all going to happen.

CHAPTER SEVEN

THE night before her wedding, only five days later, Clifford rang up. Amy took the call in the bungalow. Karen was over at the hotel dancing with Paul, and Mike was having a drink with some important guests, so she was alone.

'Amy?' Clifford sounded urgent. 'Look, I've been thinking about you. Don't rush into this marriage. It's not too late yet, and—you don't have to, Amy.'

'What do you mean?' she asked uncertainly.

There was a second's silence, then, 'You heard something about me and Margaret Leslie, didn't you?'

'Yes,' she said slowly. 'At least I—I guessed, when I rang you.'

'Well, look, Amy, I can explain it all.'

'Please, Clifford,' she interrupted, 'you don't have to explain anything. It—it doesn't matter. I'm being married tomorrow.'

'That's the whole point,' he said vehemently. 'That's why I've *got* to explain. Because you'll be making a big mistake if you go ahead with it. You don't love that guy——'

Amy didn't contradict him, she merely said wearily, 'My mind's made up, Clifford.'

'What if I tell you that Margaret and I are all washed up? Honestly, Amy, I can explain the whole thing,' he went on rapidly. 'I was sick and tired of being at the farm on my own, and I got caught up with this idea of selling out and putting the money into a business in town. I knew Margaret wanted to expand, so we sort of got together over it and—well, one thing led to another. I'm only human, and when she suggested coming to Mossman for a few weeks I naturally didn't knock it back. I suppose I got carried away, and then you turned up in the middle of it all. But it's finished now, I swear it. The whole deal's off—the partnership, the sale, everything. It's you I want. I was as jealous as hell last week when I came to Bangalo. That's when I began to realise I'd gone off my head.'

'I'm sorry, Clifford,' Amy said when he stopped speaking. 'It's too late. I can't possibly call off the wedding now. Besides, I—I don't want to.'

'I can guess why not,' he broke in bitterly. 'Mike Saunders is practically a millionaire compared to me, isn't he? But believe me, you'll regret it. Don't you care that *he's* got a mistress?'

Amy's fingers closed hard on the receiver. He meant Delona. And of course she cared. But——

'Please don't say any more,' she said coldly. 'Nothing you can say will change it—it's all decided now.'

He crashed the receiver down in her ear, and she sank trembling into the nearest chair. She felt completely shattered. Clifford wanted her back! His affair with Margaret Leslie was over. If she hadn't come to Queensland when she had, she would never even have known about it. She and Clifford would have married.

And she knew she was glad she *had* come to Queensland. All her feeling for Clifford had completely vanished; she saw him with new eyes. As for her marriage to Mike—it might well end in disaster, just as Clifford predicted. But on the other hand it just might be the most wonderful thing in the world ever to happen. She had no real idea which way it would go, but she was going to marry him. Tomorrow.

Her aunt flew up to Cairns and Mike insisted on paying her fare, though he needn't have. She, unlike Clifford, was as pleased as could be about everything. Amy had a room at the hotel for the day because the wedding was not till five o'clock, and Aunt Evelyn was to stay the night before flying back to Sydney. She told Amy with satisfaction, after she had met Mike and plainly been impressed, 'That little breather you had in Sydney this year—you see? It served a purpose! First love rarely lasts, Amy. The sugar plantation was wonderful, of course, and I knew your uncle wanted you to have it, and that's why I was happy enough about you and Clifford. But it doesn't matter—it's nothing. I'm sure you'll be happy. You'll have a full life—children, everything you could wish for. And in my opinion Michael Saunders is—well, perhaps I shouldn't say it, but he's twice the man Clifford will ever be. I'm *very* impressed.'

In a way it was an unreal wedding. There weren't many of Amy's friends there, and though the Delucas came, Clifford didn't, which she found, frankly, a relief. A few traditional tears were provided by Aunt Evelyn, and Amy knew she looked stunningly simple. Her white dress was off the peg, and it was made of very fine, very cool cotton, with a picot edge at the hem and just a touch of white embroidery on the bodice. She wore white shoes and a white hat. Mike was at his most handsome in a pale beige suit with cream silk shirt and, untraditionally, a terra-cotta tie. Paul was best man,

Karen the bridesmaid, and Amy had asked Steve to give her away, because she liked him and felt comfortable with him.

Delona, she had learned from Karen, hadn't been invited. Weddings weren't her thing.

Lucky, lucky Amy! She was well aware that most of the female guests envied her her handsome bridegroom. Outside the church, press photographers were waiting and Amy got through it all in a kind of excited dream, even though now and then she was overwhelmed by a frightened feeling that she shouldn't be doing this, that she could have stopped it all long before it was too late. She tried not to think of what lay ahead, but she wondered how many girls on their wedding day felt as uncertain as she did. Every girl who was still a virgin, possibly. She didn't dare let her thoughts linger on the coming night when she and Mike would be really alone—where, she had no idea. They weren't heading straight for Italy, at any rate, because Mike had told her, 'I don't believe in honeymoons on the move. When I take you to Italy, we'll be used to each other.'

After the reception she changed into a pale creamy dress with short sleeves, and while the guests gathered around went out to the car with Mike. It was dark by then, and everyone swarmed around the car to farewell them and to throw confetti and call out good wishes. Amy had almost expected they would be going to the airport, but instead Mike drove down to the wharves— to Trinity Inlet, past the Harbour Board Office and round to Platypus Jetty. He had a boat waiting there— a four-berth cabin cruiser, sparkling white on the outside, green in the cabin, and she looked at it with half excited, half nervous interest as he got their luggage from the car. He had told her to pack plenty of sun clothes and swimming gear—and anything else she fancied herself in, as he had put it, only this morning, on Bangalo. When she had bought her wedding dress in Cairns, she had bought a number of new clothes as well —she didn't want to wear the things she had made when she had imagined herself marrying Clifford, somehow, and after all, she had the money.

As Mike helped her aboard, her anxiety rose. Despite her clothes, despite her physical attractiveness that Mike had commented on more than once, she felt quite inadequate. She was probably the most nervous bride there ever was, and though she was now Mrs Michael Saunders, she still felt like plain Amy Martin who until a very short time ago had lived decorously with her headmistress aunt in a Sydney suburb, and dreamed of marrying Clifford North. Instead of which, here she was, married to the wealthy owner of the Hotel Bangalo and heading into the dark with him—in more ways than one—at this very minute.

'Where are we going?' she asked after he had started up the engine and they had slid discreetly from the jetty.

'You'll find out,' he said cryptically.

Amy felt enraged. Wasn't this supposed to be the age of women's liberation? So how could you possibly put up with a—a husband who treated you like that? Didn't she have a right to know where they were going? She hoped it was a long, long way—right up to the tip of Cape York—to Thursday Island maybe—so that by the time they arrived, they would both be ready for a good long night's sleep. But of course she was merely being fanciful—it would take them ages to get to Thursday Island in a boat like this and she knew very well they must be going somewhere a whole lot closer. She went down to the cabin after a moment, where she collapsed on the comfortable cushioned seat and let Mike get on with it, without demeaning herself by asking any more questions that he wouldn't answer.

There was still one question she kept asking herself, however: Why had she married him? The few days that had passed had brought her no nearer to understanding him, and she could only think *he* was marrying *her* to save himself from looking a fool. So when he grew tired of her—well, marriages were easily enough ended these days ...

The cruiser skimmed across the dark water, and exhausted as she was by the traumas of the day, she slept a little.

When she woke it was to discover they were heading for a beach that shone white in the darkness, and soon they reached a tiny jetty that bore a large notice, Private Property. There were no lights. Except for the white gleam of the sand, everything looked totally dark.

Mike helped her ashore, and weary as she was, she staggered a little. She waited while he got the luggage, then he switched on a big flashlight and she walked along the jetty to the sand, feeling very shaky and more than a little bewildered. She hadn't imagined coming somewhere so—uninhabited-looking for her honeymoon with this wealthy man, and her mind suggested crazy things—he had brought her to this lonely spot to get rid of her—she had fallen into some sort of a trap. But she was being ridiculous. Mike was a reputable and well-known man, and anyhow, what would be the point in—disposing of her? He surely couldn't hate her that much! She almost wanted to giggle, but if she began she was afraid it would end in hysteria.

She plodded across the sand with him and there among the pandanus palms, the coconuts and the tea-trees, was a house! Mike flashed his light over it—dark stained weatherboard with a sloping roof that overhung a wide verandah where there were two big squatter's chairs and a couple of tables. Soon he was opening the insect-proof door and telling her, 'Hang on a moment, Amy, and I'll get us some light.' A few moments later there was the gleam of a pretty oil-lamp, and she stared around the room into which she had stepped, and saw a spotlessly clean quarry-tiled floor, big unglazed windows with insect screens, classy-looking rattan furniture with bright cushions on the chairs, a dresser decorated with attractive pottery——

She asked unsteadily, 'Where are we?'

'You're really fooled, aren't you?' he said with a smile of satisfaction. 'Actually, we're on Bangalo—on the other side of the mountain.'

Amy nearly fell over. Bangalo! She couldn't believe it.

'Were you hoping for something more exotic—more extravagant?' he asked mockingly, and she shook her head. Yet the truth was, she *had* expected something more extravagant—and certainly more conventional. After all, Mike had put on that showy reception, and she knew well enough he had a load of money. Oh well, she thought a little dismally, he evidently didn't think her worthy of an expensive honeymoon, and for her, the thought of being totally alone with him as it looked as though she were going to be here, was more than intimidating.

Meanwhile, she looked round the room with its big windows, and the palms rustling outside in the night breeze, that brought with it the scent of frangipani blossoms, and she wondered what other rooms there were in this lonely house that was not even equipped with electricity.

She soon found out, for Mike led her on a tour of

inspection, bringing the lamp with him and lighting others as they progressed. There was a small kitchen, there was a bathroom with shower and wash-basin, there was a lavatory.

'We do have running water,' Mike told her. 'Bangalo's not short of springs. No electricity, but a septic tank and running water, which makes it comfortable enough for anyone, I should think.'

Amy nodded, following him to another room—a bedroom.

'Is there only one—bedroom?' she asked nervily, and he raised his eyebrows and looked down at her in the slightly amused yet domineering way she was getting used to.

'How many bedrooms does one need on a honeymoon?' he asked dryly. He had lighted a small lamp with a pretty pink glass shade, and now he told her, 'Hang up your things—unpack whatever you need. I'm going to get us a snack and a cold drink from the fridge.'

'The fridge?' she said eagerly—anything was better than bedroom talk.

'Yes, a kerosene fridge,' he said, and she thought, 'Like Delona has.' 'I had it stocked up ready for us. We're not going to starve, or have to forage for our food, though I hope we'll catch a few fish to add to our diet.'

He disappeared to the kitchen, leaving her alone, and she looked at the bed. Up till now, she had tried to avoid looking at it after one first quick glance. But it was hard to ignore—it was enormous, covered with a hand-painted spread in black and bronze and gold. The great windows opposite it were uncurtained, and looked through the palms and over to the sand and the sea. There were wooden shutters, but they were open, as they would be at this time of year. In the cyclone season, no doubt they would be closed.

What does one do on one's wedding night? Amy thought. But of course she knew perfectly well. It was just that she—didn't want to do it, couldn't imagine doing it. She stood at the side of the bed, biting her lip. You get undressed, you take a shower—you——

She opened her suitcase and listened to the quietness—the sea murmuring, the palms whispering, Mike moving round in the kitchen. There was a moon, and she crossed the room and looked through the windows. It had just risen, and little clouds were hurrying overhead, and the white sands were streaked with moving shadows. Amy wondered how far one would have to walk to get across the mountain and back to the hotel complex—and the airfield.

Meanwhile there was tonight to get through, and now that she was Mrs Michael Saunders, she supposed she was going to start growing up—fast ...

'Amy!' Mike's voice called imperiously.

She had taken off her shoes, and barefoot she sped to answer his call. Not because she wanted to come when he called, but because—well, she felt safer away from the bedroom. He was in the living room, and, on the long solid-looking wooden table there was an ice-bucket holding a bottle, and a flat pottery bowl containing tiny sandwiches decorated with parsley. It looked so incongruous, somehow, and she looked at Mike questioningly.

'I didn't make the sandwiches,' he admitted with a wry smile, and she sank into one of the cushioned rattan chairs, avoiding the couch. 'Would you like some champagne?'

'It would be—nice,' she said uneasily, then watched him take the bottle out of the ice and proceed expertly to draw the cork and pour champagne into two tulip-shaped glasses.

'Here's to you, Amy,' he said, raising his glass.

'To you,' she murmured in reply, then sipped the champagne and nibbled at a sandwich without much appetite.

'Well, it all went off fairly satisfactorily, don't you think, Amy?' he remarked after a few seconds.

She nodded. Their eyes met and quite suddenly she remembered his saying, 'I wouldn't like to be Clifford on your wedding night. A little bit of sex quite definitely doesn't turn you on.' The thought made her blood curdle, and she said nervily, 'It's—funny—this being our wedding night, I mean. I—I don't feel I know you at all—I don't——'

'We're going to remedy that,' said Mike, his glance enigmatic, and a shiver ran through her. She set her glass down on the table with trembling fingers. 'I can't,' she thought. 'I'll say no.' She picked up her glass and drank again to give her the courage to say it and to say it now. But how could you refuse yourself to your husband on your wedding night? It would be—cheating. And anyhow, even if she said no—— She looked at him warily over her glass. He knew all about making love, he would know how to make her give in if he really wanted her. And he had said he wanted her that way, she supposed rather vaguely. She looked round the room desperately—at the shelf of books, the transistor radio—— But you can't fill in the time with reading or listening to music indefinitely.

But it wasn't up to her to map out a plan for what they'd do, she realised, and deliberately made her mind a blank. It hurt less that way.

'Had enough to drink?' Mike asked when she had finished her champagne. 'Do you want another sandwich?' She shook her head. 'Then suppose you go along and have your shower. I'll join you presently.'

Amy stood up and went from the room obediently, her knees weak. 'Well, you're married,' she reminded herself helplessly.

She undressed in the shower room. There was no hot water, only one tap, and she stepped under the spray and shivered slightly. But the water wasn't really cold, and during the daytime, she guessed, it would be tepid or even quite warm. At any rate, it was refreshing, and she dried off on a big soft pink towel. The room was small, but the floor was tiled and there was even a cushioned bench along the wall by the basin. In the cabinet under the washbasin she found talc and body cologne, and she used the latter and stared at herself in the wall mirror, her dark eyes huge. She wore pyjamas—she had never gone in for nightgowns—and she put them on, pale yellow batiste, sleeveless and long-legged. She looked fresh and she felt fresh, and she went quietly along to the bedroom, her heart beating fast. A big moth had got in and was fluttering around the lamp. Mike had removed the bedspread from the enormous bed revealing pale blue sheets and scalloped pillow-slips to match. What did she do now? Did she get into bed? Or—or did she wait for him?

Where was he, anyhow? She could hear nothing.

She sat on the side of the bed and began brushing her hair.

It seemed centuries before he came in—bare-chested, wearing thongs and white cotton trousers.

'Where were you?' she asked.

'Did you miss me?'

She blushed. 'No, I merely wondered where you were.'

'I was taking a run along the beach.'

She looked at him, puzzled, and their eyes met. She stopped brushing her hair and simply stared. He was a stranger, but she had given him the right to make love to her today—to carry on from where he had stopped on those other few occasions when he had held her in his arms and kissed her—and she had held back and given way not a single inch.

'I'll take a shower,' he said, 'and then——'

'What?' Amy broke in, alarm in her voice. She got up from the bed and put her brush down on the chest that served as a dressing table. She tried not to look in the mirror, but she was conscious of his reflection beside her own.

'And then we'll see,' he said. And finished laconically, 'How you feel.'

Amy didn't move. 'I could tell you how I feel right now,' she thought, 'and it's not going to change. I can't possibly let you make love to me—not in cold blood.'

He came behind her silently and put his arms around her, his hands covering her breasts. Such a ripe figure, such a green girl—— Unexpectedly, she had a crazy longing to turn in his arms, to cling to him, to beg, 'Help me—help me,' but she didn't. Eyes downcast, she stayed where she was, conscious that her heart was beating fast and that Mike must feel it—conscious of the fullness of her breasts, of their warmth and heaviness through the thin material of her pyjama top against his cool hands. He bent his head and kissed the side of her neck, then he looked at her in the mirror. Her eyes were enormous, and he said sharply, 'For God's sake, Amy, don't look like that! I'm not going to rape you just because you're my legal wife—mine to do what I like with. I'm going to make love to you. And you won't need these,' he added, pinching the stuff of her pyjamas. 'You'll be a lot more comfortable if you sleep in the nude. I always do, and I don't intend altering a comfortable habit to accommodate anyone's prudishness. As well,' he added, 'you'll find two people generate a lot more heat—even in a bed the size of this one.'

Amy bit her lip, unable to meet his gaze. She had never shared a bed with anyone, and now she had no choice. He knew all about it, of course, and though she tried not to, she thought of Delona—his mistress, as Clifford had pointed out so unfeelingly.

'I shan't be long,' he said. He let his hands slide down to her waist and rest there for a moment before he turned and went to the shower room.

Amy stood undecided. She *couldn't*, she thought. Couldn't—anything. Couldn't take off her pyjamas—couldn't let him make love to her. He'd said she wasn't ready to marry anyone, and he was right. So far, in fact, she showed no signs at all of growing up, fast or otherwise.

When she heard the shower running, she went swiftly through the living room—out of the house, and down to the beach.

' I *can't*,' she muttered under her breath.

Beyond the palms, she curled up on the sand and cried a little, and then stopped. She'd read about girls being scared of sex because of some complex that went back to their childhood, but she knew perfectly well she didn't have a complex. She might be immature, but she was perfectly normal, perfectly healthy, both physically and emotionally. So she stopped crying and took a good hard look at herself. She wasn't really afraid of sex; she just hadn't thought about it a lot. Clifford had been there in her mind for so long, and for just a second she wondered why she hadn't taken the opportunity when he had rung her—and called the wedding off. But somewhere deep down she knew why not.

She sat up and hugged her knees and stared out at the dark lonely water and thought about Mike, and she remembered noticing what gorgeous teeth he had. She thought about his grey eyes and the way the hair grew on his neck. About his brown body—his chest that was smooth and tanned, his narrow hips and powerful thighs. She thought about the way he looked at her sometimes in such a—male way. And how he had taken over so absolutely—and somehow or other made her marry him. She hadn't wanted to at first, she really hadn't, but somewhere along the line she had given in —discarded Clifford and an idealistic love that had no basis in reality. Yet the fact still remained that she didn't know Mike nearly well enough for the intimacy he expected of her.

All the same, running away wasn't going to improve things, and she began to wish she hadn't disappeared from the bedroom just now. He must have finished showering by now, so—so wasn't he coming out to find her, to carry her inside and make love to her?

Apparently he wasn't.

She waited a long time, and she began to hate him. What sort of a man was he to do that—not even to come and look for her? And on their wedding night! For all he knew, she might have gone into the water and got into difficulties. She looked resentfully back at the little house among the palm trees. The light in the bedroom was still on, and she knew that he had only to look through the window to see her out here on the white beach. He probably had looked—but he was waiting for her to come to him. Well, he'd have a long wait, because she wasn't coming. The breeze from the water was growing cool, and she wondered if she built herself a wall of sand—would that help to keep her warm? Could she, in fact, stay out here all night—sleep out here? There would still be tomorrow to face, she reflected gloomily. Oh, what a fool she'd been to run away! And how unfeeling of Mike, how cruel, not to come and bring her back. If he'd come out here, taken her in his arms, by now she would have been back in the house with him, comfortable in that enormous bed and probably——

Well, she didn't know about that.

She scrambled to her feet and began walking along the sand. It was a small beach, with the little jetty at one end and a dark tangle of trees and palms at the other end. There wasn't really anywhere you could go, and she could see his footprints dark on the sand where he'd been running earlier. To keep fit, she supposed, not to—to tire himself out.

She walked more and more slowly, because she knew that when she reached the end of the beach there was nothing to do but turn round and come back again—or to sit down in the sand and feel miserable.

She plodded on, her footsteps dragging. What would Clifford think if he knew the way she was spending her wedding night? He'd think he was right, that she'd made a terrible mistake ... And Mike—what must he be thinking right now? Well, that wasn't hard to guess, either. He'd said she was a raspberry syrup kind of girl —soppy—immature. And he was right, she thought miserably. She certainly wasn't behaving like an adult.

She'd reached the end of the beach by now, and she sat down on a rock. She just wasn't going to think about anything any more. She was overtired and her head ached and she had no idea how to cope, and in another minute she would be resorting to tears again even though she knew very well that tears would get her nowhere.

Amy wept.

'You'd better come back to the house with me,' Mike's voice said from above her head.

She didn't have a handkerchief or a tissue and her face was sopping. She wiped her eyes quickly on the back of her hand and sniffed.

'How long have you been there—spying on me?'

'A couple of minutes. And you've spent quite long enough sniffling over the cruelty of life and the inescapability of becoming an adult. Come on, Amy, back to the house. I'll make you a nice hot drink and you can get into bed.'

Amy said nothing. Mike reached for her hand and pulled her to her feet, and it flashed through her mind that he was going to drag her into his arms, warm her, hold her, comfort her. But that was just what he didn't do. He wore nothing but white trousers, but his hand was warm and she knew his bare torso would be warm too—and she was cold and unhappy and lost and she'd begun to sniffle again, as he'd put it so unromantically.

He kept her hand in his as they walked back along the beach together, and she asked him, 'Does the tide come far up the beach?'

'Far enough. You'd have known all about it if you'd stayed where you were sitting earlier on,' he said succinctly. 'Is that what you were wondering? Were you hoping you might fall asleep and be blissfully drowned? I wouldn't have let it happen, I assure you.'

'You might as well have,' she said on a sob, and could almost hear him gnash his teeth.

'Now we're not going to have a howling session. You've had your little cry and I've come to the rescue and we'll take it from there. All that's wrong with you now is that you're cold—and quite unnecessarily at that. So come on—run! Run!'

Amy ran, though she didn't want to. She'd made a complete fool of herself, and Mike was probably very sorry he'd married her. The thought made her laugh weakly even while the tears ran down her face. If only she could tell him—if only she could say, 'I've been behaving like an idiot and I'm sorry'—just as if they were ordinary people in love and she was a bride with nerves on her wedding night.

'What's funny?' he asked. 'Or are you choking on your tears again?'

She didn't answer.

Back in the house, Mike lit the kerosene stove and made her a hot milk drink with sugar and a dash of rum in it, then he sent her off to bed.

Amy curled into the mattress, turned her face into the pillow and felt the utter bliss of comfort and shelter. There was only one thing missing, and that was love. She didn't turn her head when she heard him come into the room. He put out the light, and she heard him moving—divesting himself of his trousers, she thought—and then he got into bed too. Naked, she knew, because he'd said he wasn't going to change his comfortable habits for anybody, certainly not for his unwilling bride. He stayed on his own side of the bed and didn't touch her, and presently she drifted into sleep.

CHAPTER EIGHT

In the morning when she woke, Mike had gone.

She scrambled out of bed to discover where he was and deduced that he had gone out in the boat. She looked out through the big window, eager, despite the sinking feeling that last night had been a complete disaster, to see how this part of the island looked in daylight. The sea was limpid and pale and calm, sheltered by the reefs that stretched for hundreds of miles down the coast, the sky was blue and cloudless, the sunshine extravagant. She saw Mike—her husband—in faded blue shorts and a white peaked cap coming up from the beach where a small dinghy had been pulled out of the water. He was carrying some fish and she felt a crazy surge of excitement that subsided rapidly. After last night, how could she possibly rush out to meet him and admire his catch and ask what the fish were?

It was hard to restrain herself, but she managed. Instead she pretended to herself that she hadn't seen him, disappeared into the shower room, and soon reappeared wearing a long loose cotton dress she had bought in Cairns. Mike was cooking the fish, but not in the kitchen. He was outside, grilling it over a fire.

'Well, you're looking bright and chirpy this morning,' he greeted her laconically. 'What do you say to freshly caught fish for breakfast?'

'It sounds good,' she said with an effort at normalness. Should she say she was sorry about last night? Some time she must, she decided—but not just now. Not here in the shade of the palms with the enticing smell of grilling fish floating over to her and giving her an appetite. But some time she would have to let him know she wasn't going to keep on acting that way—not if he wanted something else of her. She looked up into the coconut palms and the clusters of nuts there, then kicked at a fallen nut with a bare toe. 'Would there be milk in this?'

'Sure,' he said.

She picked up the nut and shook it. 'How do you get it out?'

'When this fish is cooked, and we've eaten it, I'll show you.'

There was a bench-like table in the shade and he had brought out two chairs, spread out a red and white checked cloth and set out plates and knives and forks as well as a board with a slab of butter and some sliced bread on it.

'Civilised living,' he remarked, following her glance. 'That's for your benefit. I usually rough it when I'm living here. This little place used to belong to an eccentric entomologist. He leased this part of the island from my father. Bangalo's one of the few freehold islands on the coast—most of them are leasehold, and national parks at that. This little bungalow hadn't been used for seven or eight years when my father retired and I took over here, and I spent some time fixing it up for myself. What do you think of it?'

'It's—great,' she said uncertainly. 'I had no idea such a place existed.'

'No. Well, I keep it fairly quiet. Over the years the track through the rain forest and over the mountain has gradually been growing over, and I've let it stay that way. I don't want to make it too easy for adventurous hotel guests to invade my privacy—even a gate and keep out signs don't intimidate some people.'

The fish was ready by now, and he told Amy to sit down and prepare to enjoy something really delicious. It was coral trout, and he had cooked it to perfection, she simply couldn't fault it. They both ate with enjoyment, and it became clear that Mike wasn't going to make any reference to the previous night. While in one way she was relieved, in another it was burning a hole in her mind. She felt ashamed of her childish behaviour and longed to be able to explain it to him, though how she would do that she had no idea.

After they had finished breakfast, he showed her, as he had promised, how to get the milk from the coconut. Using a machete, he cut across the pointed end of the nut, and then kept shaving it across until the three 'eyes' were exposed. By pushing these in, one could pour out the milk.

'If the nut's sprouting,' he told her, 'it won't hold milk but *uto*, and that's a gourmet's delight. I'll let you try it some time. I'll take you into the rain forest this morning if you like, and teach you a little about my island.'

Amy accepted the offer awkwardly. It seemed a funny way to spend a honeymoon—but it was certainly no funnier than the way they had started off last night. She hoped that while they were in the rain forest, she would somehow manage to apologise for her behaviour.

She didn't, as it happened. The opportunity simply didn't come up, and besides, she was too interested in the things Mike showed her—the basket ferns, the staghorns and orchids that grew high up in the trees, the little sunbird with its nest that looked like a bundle of old leaves, and was suspended dangerously from a thin swinging vine. He showed her the strangler fig that, beginning life in a seed dropped by a bird high up in the fork of a tree, gradually grew and grew until it enmeshed its host in a cage of roots—finally strangling it to death.

The jungle, Amy discovered, was a place of both beauty and brutality, and it was as well to know what to beware of while one was admiring the butterflies or the tiny golden orchids. Mike pointed out to her the long arms of the lawyer vine that could stretch out three hundred feet or more, twining and tangling among the trees or across the paths. Escape from their curved barbs was impossible without damage to flesh and clothing, and to panic only caused more trouble. He showed her too the stinging plant, a bush with lovely heart-shaped leaves whose hairs, brushed across the skin, could cause agony that lasted for weeks.

'Why don't you have them all rooted out?' she asked, shuddering and he raised his eyebrows.

'Plants in the rain forest can be an important source of drugs, and who knows, the stinging tree may have medicinal values as yet undiscovered. It's best not to interfere with nature, Amy.'

The morning passed pleasantly and in the afternoon he took her out to the reef with him, while he fished— and promised he would take her to see the corals and the tropical fish the following day.

When they went back to the island in the evening, it was Mike who prepared the meal, which they ate outside because it was stiflingly hot indoors, and there were no big ceiling fans to cool the house down. Amy was careful not to complain about it, or even to mention it, as she felt his opinion of her was low enough already, despite the quite pleasant day they had spent together. They had fresh fruit cocktail, followed by delectably cooked crab served with salad vegetables. What happened, she wondered, when they had used up all the vegetables in the fridge? How long did Mike plan to stay on the island? When were they going to Italy? A million questions seethed in her brain, as she sat at dinner with her husband.

She ate nervously, toying with her glass, half her mind occupied with the desire to say something about the previous night. Her eyes strayed to Mike continually, to his handsome intelligent face, his hands that were strong but fine—then back to the mystery of his eyes, the windows of the soul through which she couldn't see. What did he see when he looked into her eyes? she wondered. Curiously, she found the puzzle had infinite fascination. She couldn't look away from him. She could read nothing in his face, had no idea what went on inside his head, but there was a strange delight that was almost totally sensual in merely looking into his eyes, and returning his gaze across the low table, as they sat outside in the growing dark of the tropical night.

'The dishes——' she began hesitantly when the meal was finished.

'In the morning,' he said briefly. He brought coffee and sweetish liqueurs outside, and they sat back in the rattan chairs, listening to the sea, watching the soft shadows move across the sand in a night wind that was balmy and soft. Other people were here on the island, but the world seemed a million miles away—specially as no one, so far as she knew, was aware of where they were.

After an interminable time, she said, 'Mike—last night, I—I'm sorry——'

'Think nothing of it,' he said with a shrug. 'It was more or less what I expected of you.'

She flinched, newly conscious of his contempt for her. 'You don't understand,' she said huskily, and then couldn't go on. She wanted to say, 'It's not so much that I'm afraid as that I don't know you well enough,' but she couldn't say it.

He looked at her steadily, his face unreadable in the faint moonlight. Clouds scudded across the sky so that it looked as if the moon were in flight. An illusion, Amy thought. One knew it, yet one wasn't completely persuaded. The moon was hurrying across the sky—and Mike believed she had run away from him because she was too immature to face the facts of human sexuality, yet it had been merely because she didn't know him and because—because he didn't love her, she thought with a sudden flash of understanding. She finished her coffee, gulped down her liqueur, coughed, choked, and felt a fool. And he made no comment at all.

Bedtime was looming. It couldn't be put off all night. The average honeymooner couldn't be kept away from bed, Amy supposed—morning, noon or night. But she and Mike had put in a whole day without even touching each other. She had learned a whole lot about tropical islands, but nothing at all about the human male—except that Mike was able to instruct her without letting sex intrude, and she didn't know that that was a very good sign, under the circumstances.

Bedtime. Tonight she couldn't run away. She had to stay and face up to it, and she waited passively but with growing nervousness for a lead from Mike.

'Well,' he said at last, 'are you ready for bed?'

Amy swallowed. What a question! A double-barrelled question. Her thoughts flew to the bedroom and the big bed, to her pyjamas and how he had said, 'You don't need those.' She had worn them last night all the same, but tonight——

'You're not?' he said mockingly when she didn't answer his question, didn't move. 'Then we'll go down to the beach for a while. It's hot enough. Have you ever swum in a languorous tropical sea at night, Amy?'

She shook her head. She'd never swam at night.

'It's an experience,' he promised. 'Something you'll remember all your life.' He got to his feet and stretched out a hand to her. She took it and let him pull her to her feet, and found her legs were shaking.

'I'll—I'll go and get my swimsuit.'

She heard him laugh under his breath. 'Oh no, you won't! There's no one here but you and me. What the hell do you want a swimsuit for? Now come on—tell me?'

Amy shook her head helplessly, and helplessly she let him take her down to the beach.

On the silver sands Mike stripped off his clothes with a casualness she envied, and after a moment she did the same, but feeling deeply embarrassed as she did so. Her body looked white and very naked in the moonlight and she didn't dare look at Mike, though she knew he had no qualms at all about looking at her. How much easier it would be, she caught herself thinking despairingly, if the male simply—carried you off. But this was the end of the twentieth century, and Western women didn't tolerate that kind of thing very well. 'I might,' she thought, though she wasn't at all sure.

Almost dying of embarrassment, she walked down to the water, and regardless of whether it was going to be cold or not, she walked straight into the sea and submerged. Mike followed her, then stood up, the water dripping from his head and shoulders. The sea was silky soft, the sky star-laden, and it was all suddenly unbearably beautiful and unreal. Somehow—she never really knew how it happened—she was in Mike's arms, their sea-wet bodies slippery against each other, his salt-tasting lips moving against her own. Amy had never experienced anything like the sensation of another human body touching her own in this way— totally naked, sensual, cool, smooth—wet with the waters of a warm sea. Her breasts slithered against his torso, his arms were around her drawing her closer and closer, his salty mouth parted her soft lips exploringly.

In his arms this way she knew she loved him, that she wanted him the way he had talked about wanting her, when he had agreed to the pretended engagement.

Now they were married, and waist-deep in water she clung to him, let him drink of her lips and promised heaven that she loved him and wanted to be his wife. Her hands moved of their own accord down his naked back and over his muscular buttocks as she drowned in the sweetness of his kiss.

How could it not all happen? It had to—and it was going to be so easy and so right. She was completely unresisting when Mike lifted her in his arms and carried her across the sand to the bungalow.

When she woke, very early in the morning, it was to the instant thought that she loved him and that everything had come miraculously right. And he had *been* right— she'd grown up fast——

But when she turned in the big bed she discovered with a shock that he wasn't there. She was alone. Well, he would be back presently, she comforted herself, and she lay still, feeling the smoothness of the sheet against her naked body and remembering last night. It had been like a dream, having Mike make love to her in this big bed while the palm trees whispered outside the wide insect-screened window, and cast their intricate shadows on the walls. Afterwards, when she lay exhausted in his arms, filled with the unexpected delight of physical love, she had slipped very quickly into a dreamless sleep. It was much later that she dreamed about Clifford—telling her threateningly, 'I'll tell Delona about this—about you and Mike Saunders going away together——' 'No,' she'd begged frantically, 'don't, Clifford—please don't——' She had wakened moaning, and only gradually became aware of where she really was and of the fact that she was no longer in Mike's arms. He lay on the other side of the bed, his back to her, and she had kept still, scarcely breathing,

wondering if her moans had disturbed him and if he
might misunderstand them. But his breathing was even
and with a little sigh she turned on her side and tried to
sleep again. It wasn't easy, because the memory of their
lovemaking came flooding back.

Her mad, incredible marriage was a reality now, her
whole life had changed. 'Let him love me as I love
him,' she prayed beneath her breath ...

She murmured the words again in the early morning.
Mike didn't come back to bed, and finally she got up,
realising he had gone out fishing again. She showered
and dressed, and when she went outside he had breakfast almost ready—fresh fish again, fruit, and coffee.
But though she had imagined he would more or less
drop everything when she appeared—come to take her
in his arms and kiss her—he did no such thing.

'Good morning, Amy.' His greeting was cool and
careless, though his eyes skimmed down her figure in
the plain white dress, taking in her bare feet, then returning to her gleaming dark hair and her unpainted
lips—ready to be kissed.

'You've been out fishing,' she exclaimed. 'Why
didn't you wake me? I could have come too.'

He looked at her enigmatically. 'I was up very early.
And I didn't care to wake you—you looked completely
happy with your dreams, whatever they were.'

She coloured slightly, uneasy at something in his
tone, then sat down and helped herself to pawpaw.

'The best of all tropical fruits,' he remarked, joining
her. 'It's supposed to make women beautiful and men
virile.'

'Is it?' Amy said inadequately. The remark was a
little too sophisticated for her, and she continued to eat
her breakfast without talking, though now and again
she glanced across at him—taking in with new eyes the

texture of his hair, the brown of his skin, the way his lashes curled up and were unexpectedly gold-tipped. But she didn't once catch his eye, and her feeling of unease gradually deepened. She wished he would say something tender, or come round the table to kiss her —or simply reach across to touch her hand. *She* wanted to do those things, but she hadn't the self-confidence.

Finally he got up from the table and said briskly, 'When you're ready, I'll take you out on the reef. But don't be too long. If it's to be worthwhile we must be there at low water. Make sure you wear rubber shoes or sandshoes. We'll be walking on the reef and you don't want to cut your feet or tread on a stonefish. Put on a long-sleeved shirt if you have one, and a hat.'

'Yes, Mike,' she said, her voice low, and he looked at her sharply. Her mouth trembled slightly and tears were not far away. She couldn't understand his complete impersonality. It was—it was a kind of insult, somehow, and as he turned away and went to make his own preparations, two tears ran down her cheeks. Bliss last night, and now hurt. Deep, deep hurt—and Mike wasn't even aware of it. But then, she thought bitterly, he was a husband who didn't love his wife. Her prayers had plainly been in vain.

They went out to the reef in the dinghy—out over the calm pale-coloured sheltered waters, until they reached the Barrier Reef, its strangely flattish surface almost totally exposed by the low tide, and only gently washed over by the sea. Mike secured the boat and they walked across to the far side, where Amy could see the waves washing it, making waterfalls as they ran back over the reef. Branched corals grew in the blue waters on the ocean side of the reef, and limey plants gave the edges pink and purple colouring. Further back were big coral boulders, broken from the reef by the sea and thrown beyond the reach of the waves, there to provide shelter for numerous creatures. Mike moved several of them—later putting them back again—so that she could see the starfish and crabs and various molluscs that hid underneath.

But best of all was when they came back towards the reef channel where there were big pools. Here the water was so completely clear and still it seemed not to exist at all. The beautiful many-coloured many-shaped corals, the anemones and fish there could be seen with a crystalline clarity, and Amy forgot everything else as she stared fascinated. When Mike touched the expanded green polyps of a red pipe organ coral, so that they contracted to reveal the brilliant red skeleton beneath, she exclaimed in delight. And just as much she enjoyed watching the little vermilion and white clown fish, that darted about among the stinging tentacles of a huge carnivorous anemone.

'They're messmates,' Mike told her. 'I believe they lure other fish in, but for some reason they're immune themselves to the anemone's poison.'

They were almost back to the dinghy when he showed her the dreaded stonefish, barely distinguishable as it lay sluggishly at the bottom of a big rock pool.

'That's why you wear shoes around the reef,' he said. 'Tread on one of those by mistake and thirteen deadly spines will rise from its back and fill you with poison— and it's a long way to go for the effective treatment that has at last been developed.'

The reef was like the rain forest, Amy decided as she climbed back into the dinghy. Beautiful but frightening as well. She was filled with a sense of wonder, and she began to think hopefully that she had imagined the coldness between them this morning. Mike had been so pleasant, so informative—he couldn't have been nicer.

'Mike——' she began uncertainly as they started back towards Bangalo.

'Well?'

She froze instantly at the harshness of his tone. He was a stranger again, she hadn't been imagining things.

'Nothing,' she said, shaking her head and looking away from him.

'Say it,' he said almost savagely. 'Come on, say what's on your mind.'

She bit her lip. Say, Why aren't you being nicer to me? Say, I love you. Say, Was I a disappointment to you last night? Say, Teach me and I'll try to please you—— No, she couldn't say any of those things, not now. She said shakily, 'Later—I—not now.'

He didn't press her, but she felt his look of contempt and she felt despair. *Why?*

After lunch she went into the bedroom to lie on the bed and rest, worn out by the morning on the reef. It was coolish there, though she missed the big ceiling fans, and in no time she fell asleep, sprawled on top of the big bed, in a loose cotton dress.

When she woke she lay thinking of Mike—thinking of his coolness, of the lack of communication between them. It was something she couldn't take for long, and it had completely spoiled the beauty of her surrender to him the night before. What kind of a man was he? she wondered. Didn't he understand a woman's sensitivity in these things? Did he take sex so much for granted he didn't realise what impact her first experience of it had made on her?

Or was it that he simply didn't care one way or the other about the girl who was Amy Martin? Her body— yes, her body gave him pleasure, though apparently not enough—but she herself meant nothing to him.

Restlessly, she got up from the bed and went to look for him. Honeymoons were notoriously difficult—she'd read that in magazines—and if there were anything she could do to improve their relationship, then she'd do it. *Anything*.

She couldn't find him. And she discovered with a little chill of fear that the cruiser had gone.

So he'd gone fishing, she told herself, that was all.

'I'll give him a great big welcome when he comes back,' she decided. 'I'll find some flowers to put in the house—I'll make something specially nice to go with the fish. I'll make myself look really pretty. He won't possibly be able to go on being so impersonal and distant. And tonight—in bed—I'll tell him how I feel.'

She stood on the verandah as these thoughts chased each other hopefully through her head, and she heard the soft thud as a coconut dropped on the ground. In the rain forest behind the house, the sulphur-crested cockatoos were screeching and there was another high-pitched sound that Mike had told her was the fruit bats, high in the trees. They quarrelled and shrieked half the day, but at night they were quiet as they flew off to their hunting grounds in search of food.

Amy went outside barefooted and picked some yellow and pink hibiscus flowers to put in a bowl, then she inspected the contents of the fridge and the food cupboard. There were salad vegetables, green beans and onions, and she found rice and a variety of spices. She'd cook rice, she thought, and make a Chinese sauce that would go well with fish.

In her bedroom, she took a really beautiful leisure gown from the wardrobe. It was one she had bought in Cairns and there was a touch of the primitive about its black and gold and red. She'd wear that, and put her hair up some way—not too formally, she thought, experimenting in front of the mirror. There must be some way you could put your hair up that would make a man want to pull it down—and make love to you, she added under her breath. Because that was what she wanted, a little to her shame. Yet whatever she looked like, he would probably do that—simply because he was a man and he had the right.

The sun was going down spectacularly by the time she had everything ready in the kitchen and was dressed as she had planned. But Mike hadn't come, and she began to feel so tensed up she wanted to scream. Had something awful happened to him? But it couldn't have —he wasn't the kind of man to have accidents, she told herself firmly.

It grew pitch dark, and then the moon rose, gilded and beautiful among the flitting clouds, and made the beach into a romantic, magic place. But Amy, in her pretty dress, and with her hair pinned up and ready to tumble down if just one pin were withdrawn, paced along the sand with nothing but her own shadow to keep her company. She could have wept, but what was the use of crying?

Mike didn't come, and she didn't know what time it was when she eventually went inside, stripped off her dress, got into her pyjamas and curled up wide-eyed and miserable on top of the sheet, sure she would never sleep.

She did, of course—and woke early in the morning to the sound of thunder. She sat up instantly. Nobody in the bed beside her—and when she looked along the beach, where she had run still in her pyjamas, there was still no boat at the jetty. The dinghy had been pulled up on the sand yesterday and was still there— but she couldn't use it. She had no idea how to start up a car, let alone an outboard motor, and she hated herself for her uselessness. Because she knew she should go for help—she was quite convinced by now that something *had* happened to Mike. Otherwise he'd have been back.

The sky had grown blacker, and the sea looked grey and angry, and thunder growled again as she ran inside to get into jeans and shirt and sandals, and with a feeling that was close to panic hurried round the house to the jungle behind it. In sunshine, it was cool and romantic, but this morning, with heavy clouds rolling in from the sea, it was dark and hostile and frightening. With some difficulty she found the overgrown path that Mike had said went through the rain forest and over the mountain to the hotel on the other side. She had to get help—to tell Paul and Karen that Mike was missing—to get a search party out—and she started along it fearfully. The dim light was sinister, and the tall, huge-trunked trees seemed to reach up for ever to a sky that she couldn't even see, draped with looping vines that looked like hundreds of feet of hangman's rope. And across the tangled path, other vines twisted and writhed like the coils of some giant python.

Amy pushed her way on, stopping now and again to try to distinguish signs of a path, sobbing a little as she thought of Mike and what could have happened to him—wishing now she had gone for help last night instead of waiting till this morning. But she would never have found her way in the dark—it was bad enough in daylight, such as it was.

The thunder began again, terrifyingly close, and straight overhead the sky was split open by a tremendous blinding flash of lightning. It was then that she blundered into the savage clutches of a lawyer vine, perhaps torn loose by the wind that had begun to rage through the forest as the first huge soaking drops of rain came down. It was as though invisible and vicious claws had seized her by the throat, and in less than a second she was completely trapped by the wickedly barbed thorns of the vine. 'If you struggle,' Mike had told her, 'so much the worse for you.' But Amy couldn't help it. She completely lost her head as she tried to escape. She screamed and screamed again, and felt the searing pain as a thousand sharp thorns tore her flesh and her clothes while she struggled senselessly to free herself.

And suddenly above her own screams she heard someone shouting her name.

She stood quite still, petrified, eyes wide, listening —sure she'd imagined it. She was only half aware of the sting of the thorns pressing into her flesh—her arms, her ribs, her breast, even the lower part of her face. All she could hear was the shrieking of cockatoos as the rain poured down and slid in torrents from the trees. And then the voice came again.

'Amy!'

'Here!' she screamed. 'I'm here—oh, Mike, help me—help me——'

Seconds later she heard him crashing through the rain forest, and now she was fully conscious of the excruciating agony in her body as the lawyer vine held on to her as if it would never let her go. Bangalo Island didn't want her here, she was an intruder—an alien—

She twisted round when he came, tears of relief and pain on her face.

'For God's sake keep still!' he rapped out, and she obeyed instantly, standing stiffly and trying not to tremble.

It took him a long time to free her, and he swore often, telling her innumerable times, 'Stand still, damn you—you're not helping either of us wriggling about like that.'

Then when at last she was free and fully conscious of her torn flesh and the thorns embedded in it, he asked her furiously, 'What the hell are you doing messing about here in the storm, anyhow? Where did you think you were going?'

'To the hotel,' she quavered, though she meant to say it indignantly.

'For heaven's sake, why?'

'You—you don't think I've been exactly enjoying myself, do you—wondering where you were?' It was insane, but her relief at seeing him again was completely swamped by other stronger feelings—resentment that he should be so angry with her, hurt that he didn't seem aware she would have been worried. The rain still fell down, the thunder was receding, the jungle pressed in dark and green but not now so menacingly.

'You'd never have got through to the hotel in a million years,' Mike told her with harsh scorn. 'Haven't you got any brains? Didn't you listen to what I told you the other day?' He had taken hold of her arm and was hustling her along as he made his way back along the path by which he had come. 'Why do you imagine I told you about the lawyer vine? Did you doubt my word? Did you have to find out for yourself?'

'What do you think?' Amy snapped back. Her teeth were chattering, but it was certainly not from cold. It was from anger and agony—and from hate as well. Why had she ever imagined she had fallen in love with this hateful hard brute of a man whom she had—heaven forgive her!—married? 'Did you imagine I was going to stay at the house indefinitely while you——'

He thrust aside a dripping green fern-frond and

pushed her ahead of him along the path, and she almost tripped over a thick vine. Unsympathetically Mike grabbed hold of her and kept her upright. 'You had only to use your head to realise I must have had trouble with the boat. I'm not in the habit of leaving girls stranded indefinitely.'

'Aren't you?' she said indignantly. 'Well, how am I to know that? I—I have no idea what sort of things you're in the habit of doing. Where were you, anyhow?'

'I had some business to do at the hotel,' he said tersely. 'Now shut up and look where you're going. I don't want to waste time disentangling you from any more vines—it's going to take an hour to fix you up when we get back home as it is.'

'You needn't bother,' she muttered through her teeth. 'I'll survive.' She blundered on ahead of him recklessly, keeping out of his reach, thrust aside a dripping branch, and ducked her head just in time to avoid one of those hooked vines.

With an impatient exclamation he pushed past her. 'You'd better follow me, you fool of a girl. It's a wonder you made it as far as you did. Next thing, you're going to sprain your ankle when you trip over something.'

That was highly likely, because by now she was blinded by tears. The rain had suddenly ceased, and a brilliant beam of sunlight came through the trees, and flitting along in it carelessly was a turquoise blue butterfly. Amy blinked her tears away and watched it, her mouth falling open in dismay as the beautiful creature was unexpectedly caught in a spider's web.

'That's a bird-eating spider's web,' Mike told her, and she thought he sounded unbearably callous. 'It's like me,' she thought. 'I'm caught in a web'—and she didn't know if it was a web of hate or a web of love.

Everything was steaming when they eventually emerged from the rain forest into the clearing round the bungalow. Beyond the palms, the sea was a sparkling blue, and water dripped in glittering crystal drops from the lovely battered heads of the hibiscus flowers, and the air was full of a bruised fragrance. Mike waited for Amy to go up to the house with him, his eyes running over her clinically. What a sight she must look, she thought, her white jeans muddy, her hair bedraggled, her shirt torn. And she'd made herself so beautiful for him last night! Well, she was glad he hadn't turned up. She didn't want to look beautiful for him. She hated him. Marrying as she had done was the stupidest act of her whole life.

'Go inside to the bedroom and get your clothes off,' Mike ordered shortly. 'I'll see what I can do about those thorns, but you're going to have to put up with a lot in the next few days, and you'll have to make up your mind to it.'

She looked at him silently. Thorns in the flesh were nothing compared with being married to him—cooped up here alone with him, she thought, absentmindedly noting the pile of passion-fruits and pawpaws on the verandah table.

'How much longer are we staying in this hateful place?' she heard herself ask querulously, and his jaw hardened.

'That depends,' he said harshly. 'Why? Do you want to get away from me so urgently? Is that what you were doing this morning—trying to run away and get back to the mainland?'

'Maybe I was,' she said. She reached out and idly picked up a couple of passion-fruit—purplish brown and glossy, and smelling delicious—and dropped them suddenly as though they'd burned her. That fruit!

Delona had given them passion-fruit and pawpaws from her garden the day they visited Nerina.

Her eyes went to Mike with sudden understanding. 'You've been with Delona, haven't you?' she accused.

He looked back at her icily, his grey eyes dark and unfeeling, then he smiled twistedly.

'You want to think I've been unfaithful to you, do you? Is that to excuse your own guilt?'

'What do you mean?' she asked, bewildered. 'I—I haven't seen anyone—not anyone but you.'

'I know that. But haven't you been wishing I were Clifford—weren't you imagining that when we made love the other night?'

She turned her head away, confused by his mentioning their lovemaking.

'How could I ever imagine you were Clifford?' she said huskily. 'You're not in the least like him. You're—you're brutal!' she finished vehemently.

'You found my lovemaking brutal?' he asked after a frozen instant. His voice was laconic, drawling, but there was something behind the laziness that made her shiver inwardly. He didn't like what she had said —and of course she hadn't been referring to his lovemaking—it was just the way he was treating her today. 'If that's the way you felt about it, Amy, then it's a bloody shame no one ever made love to you before I did. Because I tell you in real life you'd find your— *dream lover* brutal if you found me so.'

'My dream lover?' she repeated dazedly.

'Clifford North,' he said exasperatedly. 'And for your information, I definitely don't like the feeling I'm being confused with another man when I'm making love —and being called by his name when it's over.'

'But I—I didn't——'

'You did,' he said coldly. 'And now are you going to

do as I told you? Go in and get those clothes off.'

She turned away and went inside, past the drooping hibiscus flowers she had arranged so hopefully last night, and into the bedroom. Had she really called him Clifford? She couldn't believe it—unless she'd had that dream sooner than she'd believed. She stood irresolute in the middle of the room, feeling desperately unhappy. How could she take her clothes off—have Mike attending to the cuts and scratches on her body—her breast, her stomach? She looked at her arms, seeing the vicious little dark barbs lodged in the flesh under the dried streaks of blood, and knew she couldn't possibly deal with them herself.

Mike came into the room to find her still standing there. He had a bowl of water, some antiseptic, tweezers, a needle, cotton wool.

'What's the matter? Is my brutality worrying you? Do you think I'm going to hurt you deliberately?' He set the bowl down on the top of a chest as he spoke and came towards her purposefully. Amy didn't answer his questions, but with a feeling of fatality she turned away and peeled off her wet shirt, then unfastened her bra. Mike knew a lot about her body by now; it was pointless to feel she wanted to hide it from him.

'Your pants too,' he said mockingly, as she moved to sit down on the side of the bed. 'Apart from anything else, they're wet.'

Mutely, she unzipped her jeans and pulled them off, then sat down in her panty briefs and waited, not looking at him, for him to attend to her injuries.

He worked methodically and carefully at extracting the thorns from her flesh for some minutes. He was infinitely gentle, and completely impersonal. It seemed as if her breast was no more to him than her arm, and gradually her inner trembling vanished and she relaxed.

It was while he was dealing with her shoulder that he said, 'I suppose you want to know what happened last night.'

All her nervousness came back. 'You don't have to tell me.'

'On the contrary, I think I do have to tell you, otherwise you'll be imagining a lot of things that didn't happen ... After I'd seen Paul, I went over to Nerina to see how Delona's progressing with her work for the exhibition.' He paused as though to give her a chance to attack him over that, but she said nothing. The exhibition was only an excuse, but who was she to contest it? 'Around sundown, when I was ready to leave, I discovered I had motor trouble—quite serious trouble, something that was going to take me hours to deal with.'

'All night?' Amy couldn't help putting in bitterly.

'Possibly,' he said icily, 'under the circumstances existing on Nerina ... However, Delona was expecting Harry—who runs the bar at the hotel, you might remember—to come over with some stuff for her, and I decided I'd get him to bring me across here. Unfortunately, he didn't turn up, so I stayed the night and got up at dawn to work on my motor.'

'I see,' said Amy, her voice quivering. She didn't believe for an instant that Delona had been expecting Harry—she might have said she was, and Mike *might* have believed her. She wanted to ask, 'And what happened during the night? Where did you sleep?' but she didn't. The answers were obvious—and of course he wouldn't tell her the truth.

She sat still while he finished doing what he could about her wounds, and she felt sore and miserable. She felt sick too, partly from hunger, because she'd eaten practically nothing since lunchtime the day before. When Mike had finished, he stood looking down at her and she felt herself sway slightly.

'Was it that bad? Are you going to pass out? Lie down, for heaven's sake—why didn't you tell me you felt like that? I'll get you some brandy.'

Amy collapsed weakly on the bed, and a minute later he came with the brandy. She felt his arm against her bare flesh as he raised her a little and made her drink.

'I'm all right,' she said with a pale smile. 'I'm hungry, I guess.'

'No breakfast?' She shook her head. 'I'll get you some coffee—and I've brought some fresh bread.'

When he disappeared she forced herself to get up and dress, though she dispensed with a bra out of consideration for her scratches. She would have liked a shower, but that would wash off all the disinfectant Mike had applied, so it would have to wait till later. Her hair had dried and it looked any old how, and she damped it and ran a comb through it wearily. She didn't think she was going to finish up looking particularly seductive, and she didn't really want to. And to think Mike had had the effrontery to ask if she were trying to excuse her own guilt! He must have heard her moaning Clifford's name in her sleep, but it didn't seem to matter much one way or the other. Obviously they weren't going to make a success of their marriage when he had gone back to his mistress before the honeymoon was anything like over! Clifford had been right—she had made a big mistake.

She was wishing she hadn't married him as she went out to the kitchen for her coffee, and then, when he looked up at her, his eyes momentarily soft and—caring, one would almost have thought, she felt a weakness in her limbs and knew that she didn't really wish it at all. She knew that she wanted him to love her—more than she'd ever wanted anything in her life before. But of course, he didn't.

'Cracking hardy?' he asked with a lift of his brows. 'I'd have brought this in to you.'

'The brandy's made me feel better,' she said with an attempt at brightness.

'We'll take it outside,' he said. He had buttered some bread, piled pawpaw on to a dish, made coffee, and meekly she followed him on to the terrace.

After she had eaten, she spent the rest of the morning sleeping in the shade while Mike sat nearby, reading. And thinking, she supposed, of Delona.

She couldn't for the life of her imagine why he had married her.

CHAPTER NINE

MIKE offered to take her out fishing with him in the boat during the afternoon.

'That way you can be quite sure where I am,' he said cynically, and though Amy had been on the point of accepting, that remark made her change her mind and she refused.

When he had gone, she wandered along the beach picking up shells and pieces of broken coral, her heart sore, her mind troubled. Their marriage was impossible and she had no idea what to do about it. The thought of sharing him with Delona was unbearable, and though she had known about Delona from the start, she hadn't thought it would be like this. She certainly hadn't imagined he would spend a night with her during their honeymoon! She knew she must assure him that she had got over Clifford, but to convince him of it was going to be a very different matter, she reflected unhappily.

This time he was back on the island before sundown. He had caught some fish, and he was very polite and agreeable when she offered to make a sauce to go with it. Later, as they ate their meal by lamplight on the wide verandah, he even praised her for it. Perhaps he was intent on showing her that he wasn't brutal, or perhaps he was being nice to her because he realised she was still sore from her battle with the lawyer vine. In any case, of one thing she was quite certain: he wouldn't attempt to make love to her tonight.

However, she was wrong.

They went for a walk along the beach after dinner and made conversation about the storm and the way it had disappeared without a trace, except for the fact that a few flowers were battered, a few branches broken, a few extra coconuts had fallen. In the face of Mike's polite impersonality, it was impossible to introduce the subject of Clifford, and finally, in despair, Amy excused herself and went inside to bed. Perhaps later, in bed, she could somehow tell him. That was, if he came in before she was asleep, and she suspected that he wouldn't.

She undressed and showered. The cuts and scratches on her arms and face didn't look too bad, but there was an ugly red mark across the tender skin of her right breast. She considered looking for the ointment, then changed her mind. Mike had lit the bedroom lamp earlier and she had just decided to put it out and get into bed when he appeared in the room. He was barefooted and wore nothing but white shorts that showed the power of his muscular body, and his tanned legs and arms.

'Did you put some of that cream on your cuts?' he demanded.

She shrugged, colouring slightly under his gaze. 'I'm very healthy—they'll heal.'

'They'll heal a whole lot faster and you'll be much more comfortable if you treat them instead of leaving it all to nature,' he said roughly, then added mockingly, 'Or were you waiting for me?'

Her nerves jumped and she had to swallow before she answered. 'No. I—I don't need you to look after me.'

'I'm going to do it just the same,' he said tersely. He disappeared to the bathroom and was back in seconds, the small jar of ointment in his hand. Amy knew perfectly well he expected her to take off her pyjama jacket, but she quite literally couldn't do it. It was—different tonight from the way it had been this morning. She felt intensely aware of him as a man—as, ridiculously, her husband. And she was nervously conscious of the fact that he was in the mood for making love. How she knew this she wasn't quite certain. It might have been the way he was looking at her, or something in his expression, or even in the tone of his voice.

So she wasn't really surprised when he suddenly crossed the room, unbuttoned her pyjama jacket and pulled it open, revealing her breasts—one white and smooth, the other marred by an angry red line, thickened at intervals by darker marks where the thorns had been. He raised his eyes to hers, then deliberately removed her jacket, tossing it on to the bed, and then he took her in his arms, crushing her breast against the bare flesh of his chest.

Amy felt a shiver of anticipation run through her, and unconsciously she raised her face to his and felt the hardness of his mouth come down on her own. It was an electrifying moment, and she wanted with all her being to respond. Yet she couldn't. Even as she tasted his lips she thought of Delona and something in her froze. Last night Mike had held Delona's naked body in his arms—made love to her. She knew he had, it was inevitable, alone with her as he had been——

She felt herself stiffening, then she broke away from him fiercely, unable to bear the close physical contact any longer.

'What's the matter?' he asked harshly. 'Are you afraid of my—brutality? Or can't you get your ex-fiancé out of your mind?'

She turned her back on him, crossing her arms over her bare breast. 'I'm not—I'm not always thinking about Clifford. I told you so—why can't you believe me?'

He seized her by the shoulders and swung her round to him again. 'How can I believe you when even in your sleep you mumble his name?'

'But I—I can't help that,' she protested weakly. 'It was just a dream.'

'Then it's time you stopped dreaming and faced up to a few facts, Amy mine. Whether you like it or not, you're married to me and you'll have to get used to it. It's no use continuing your girlish fantasies about a man who's found himself a woman he likes better than you. Besides, he can hardly manage two women at once, you know.'

His eyes looked into hers inscrutably, and she thought painfully of Delona. Did he think *he* could

manage two women at once? Because he couldn't—
she wouldn't stand for it. It might amuse Delona, but
not her. Her morals were rather old-fashioned.

And as for Clifford——

'Clifford hasn't another girl-friend, as it happens,'
she said.

Mike's eyes bored into her and his hands moved on
her shoulders, the thumbs pressing bruisingly into her
flesh, so that if she hadn't thought him brutal before,
she was beginning to now.

'What the hell are you trying to tell me? Was that
all a lie—that he'd found someone else? Was it all a
trick——'

'No,' she said chokingly, and winced as his hold on
her grew even more hurtful. 'He's—it's over. Clifford
rang me——'

'When?'

'The—the night before the wedding.'

'He wanted you back.'

'Yes,' she whispered, her face paling.

'Then why didn't you go?' he said violently. 'Half a
wife is no use to me.'

He sounded as if he wished she *had* gone, and she
knew very well why she hadn't. It had been because
deep down she knew she was more in love with him
than she had ever been with Clifford. But how could
she tell him that?

She said unevenly, 'You—you threatened me no girl
would ever walk out on you.'

'I *threatened* you?' he repeated. 'You mean you
thought I'd have—dragged you to the altar? Killed
Clifford before I let him take you away from me?' His
voice was savage, and she didn't answer. She saw his
eyes narrow and a muscle tighten in his jaw. 'Or were
you—saving my feelings the way you saved Clifford's,

when you told him I wanted to marry you? If so, I'm afraid I don't appreciate that kind of sacrifice, Amy. If you'd come to me, I'd have told you to go—but fast!'

The way Clifford had told her to go, she thought, shocked and trembling in his grasp.

The next instant he had flung her down on the bed, and for a moment, as he stared down at her, his eyes glittering, his brows drawn, she was sure he was going to rape her. Then he picked up her pyjama jacket and tossed it over her.

'I'm going to sleep on the boat. You can have all your dreams to yourself.'

He flung off, and shaking, Amy watched him go from the room—heard the screen door slam as he went outside, heard his footsteps on the path. She lay where she was, feeling more unhappy than she had ever felt in her life. Was this the sort of trauma one could expect to go through on a honeymoon? Of course it wasn't—it couldn't be. Normal people started off loving each other, understanding each other. She and Mike had started from nothing. So what could she have expected, fool that she was?

She put out the light and got into bed. The ointment was still on the chest, but she hadn't used it and she didn't care. All the same, it wasn't physical pain that kept her awake. She couldn't stop thinking of Mike and of the things they had said to each other. It was painfully clear he regretted having married her, and she knew he must be comparing her very unfavourably with Delona.

Was he out there on the boat? she wondered. Or had he gone over to Nerina? If he had, she could hardly blame him, but the thought was agony. She watched the shadows of the palms move slowly across the room, and she couldn't sleep. At last she could stand it no more. She went out to the verandah, wearing only her pyjama pants, for she hadn't bothered to put on the jacket again. In the moonlight she could see the jetty, and the shimmer of the white cruiser against the still darkness of the water.

She went back to bed and at last she slept.

Mike came back to the bungalow in the morning. Amy had seen him swimming when she'd got up, dark shadows round her eyes, her head aching. She had made coffee, cut some of the bread he had brought back the day before, sliced up a pawpaw and squeezed a little orange juice over it. Just like a wife—a loving bride, she thought bitterly. They ate together outside in the cool of the morning, Mike bare from the waist up, Amy in a loose cotton dress, desperately unhappy and trying not to show it.

She was shocked when, after they had both finished eating, he said abruptly, 'You'd better go back to your old boy-friend. I can't live with a rag doll for a wife, and I'm afraid that's what you are, Amy.'

The colour slowly left her face, and she stared at him, her throat dry. Pack up and go—was that what he meant? Just like that. No more talk, no more fights— The end.

He got up from his chair and walked a few paces in the shade of the palm trees, then came back to stand by the table and look at her darkly.

'Why the hell did you marry me? For my name— for my money?'

She could have said, Because I fell in love with you, but how could she expect him ever to believe that? She was beginning to find it difficult to believe herself, and yet it was true, true, true.

She said, her voice high-pitched and just slightly

hysterical, 'Well, what do you think?'

He looked at her intently, his eyes narrowing, and she looked back at him. Then he said slowly, 'Is this by any chance something you and Clifford have dreamed up between you? Are you—like my sister's husband appears to be doing—planning to get what you can out of me, maybe a nice big fat lump sum, and then—disappear?'

It was like a nightmare, and every time she spoke she seemed to make it worse, but she shook her head, biting her lip. Mike took no notice at all of her denial as he swept on.

'You're not quite as innocent as you look, are you? Well, I've had the first taste of you. You won't be the frightened little virgin you were by the time Clifford gets you into his bed. I have a good mind to give you a little more experience before I let you go—you've certainly asked for it!'

'I—I haven't!' she gasped protestingly. 'And—and why did you marry *me*, anyway, when you can have Delona Ferguson? Will *you* care if we get a divorce at the end of twelve months? You'll be able to marry her then, won't you? She'll have her divorce then too——'

He ran his fingers through his hair with a weary gesture. 'You've got it all wrong, Amy. Delona's not getting a divorce—ever.'

Amy leaned limply back in her chair. That, she thought, answered a lot of questions. He couldn't marry Delona. And a man in his position needed a—a legal wife, legitimate children. But he'd made a mistake in choosing her—it had all fallen to pieces, though she still wasn't really sure how it had all happened.

'I'll go over to the hotel this afternoon,' Mike said after a moment. 'Finalise a few details with Paul. He's going to manage the place when we go to Italy. Our flight's been booked, but I'll cancel yours, once we get to the mainland. You can do as you please, then. I'll go to Italy. Maybe I'll stay on in Europe for a while. It will all blow over, as you suggested so wisely it would, some time ago.'

Amy listened to him, frozen. She longed to be able to say something that would put it all right, but it wasn't nearly as simple as that.

'Well?' he drawled, his voice icy. 'Do you agree?'

She shook her head helplessly. 'But we—we're married, Mike,' she said brokenly, and he laughed harshly.

'You don't know what marriage is, Amy. You've lost your virginity, that's all.'

It wasn't all, of course. She'd lost her heart as well, and no matter what happened, she could never go back to Clifford. Nothing could ever be the same again. It would be easier for Mike. He would find another girl to marry him—a mature girl who would know how to satisfy him in bed so that he wouldn't need to run off to Delona Ferguson on her lonely island any more.

That afternoon Mike took the boat over to the other side of the island, leaving Amy to pack her belongings and to reflect bewilderedly that her marriage was over before it had even begun. There seemed nothing she could do about it. A man like Mike would have no hesitation in taking positive action—leaving her, getting on with his own preparations for a new life. As for her, she had no idea what she would do when he had gone. To go back to Clifford was totally out of the question. He had asked her to come back to him, but she didn't really believe in his love. He had been more wrapped up in Margaret Leslie than he had ever been in her. The idea of going back to Aunt Evelyn didn't appeal either. What was she going to think about all this, anyhow? She had been so pleased about the marriage, it would be a shock to her to know it was a complete failure. It simply didn't bear thinking about. Karen too—what would she have to say? Amy felt she couldn't bear to see any of them again for a long time. It would be easier for Mike, away in Europe ...

'Everything's arranged,' he told her when he came back to the house. 'I've managed to get a flight to Italy in two days' time, so we'll leave here tomorrow. It's pointless to stay any longer. The sooner we make the break the better.'

His tone was brisk and impersonal, and Amy supposed he was right. It was no use protesting, and she merely asked quietly, 'Shall I clean out the house—empty the fridge—the food cupboards?'

'Forget all that. I've fixed up for someone to come and see to all that tomorrow afternoon, after we've gone. All you need do is pack up your own things.'

They ate, but she had no idea what they ate, then Mike sat in one of the squatter's chairs on the verandah reading and ignoring her. Amy showered, put some ointment on her scratches, then got into her pyjamas, put out the light, and climbed into bed. What a marriage! He had said it wasn't a marriage at all, yet for her it had been. She began to pray for a miracle to happen—for Mike to come to bed—for them to make love —for him to discover somehow that he couldn't let her go after all.

But she broke off in the middle of her prayer. It was no use hoping for the impossible.

She didn't know how Mike spent the night, but he certainly didn't come to sleep in the big bed where she lay. She slept so lightly and she woke so often she would have known if he had come into the room. Perhaps he slept on the boat, and perhaps he didn't sleep at all.

She couldn't eat a thing in the morning, and while Mike had his usual breakfast she stayed in the bedroom, packing her things. When it was all done, she stood at the window looking outside for the last time. She would remember this place for ever, she thought —this island paradise, this secret hideaway. And she would remember for ever the hard lesson she had learned here. The game, if one could call it that, had certainly proved to be rough!

She was about to turn away when she saw a boat coming in at the jetty, and stared in disbelief. Presently a man and a girl appeared, and as they walked towards the beach she recognised them as Paul and Karen. What on earth were they doing here? Her heart began to pound. Had Mike told them in confidence about the split-up? Was Karen coming to see if she could do something about it? Oh, Amy hoped not. She didn't think she could bear the trauma of having other people interfere in what was so personal and complex—and incomprehensible—a matter.

Mike had seen the visitors too, for he appeared outside the house beyond the verandah, and after a moment Amy hurried out to join him.

He turned his head and looked at her enigmatically. 'It appears we have visitors. Shall we keep up the fiction of being happy honeymooners, or would you rather parade our failure?'

'You—you didn't tell them?' she asked jerkily.

'Of course not,' he said abruptly. He put an arm around her as he spoke and she flinched—because he'd brushed against one of her tender spots, though he misinterpreted her reaction. 'I'm sorry if my touch is so distasteful to you, but you'll have to put up with it unless you've decided to settle for telling all.'

'No, I'd rather we didn't,' she said quickly, and

added under her breath, 'I—I don't find your touch distasteful. It's just the—the lawyer vine.'

'My apologies,' Mike said dryly, and removed his arm though he stayed close to her. 'I must have forgotten to give Paul instructions about something important that they're coming here to invade our privacy.'

'It hardly matters now,' she said wearily. 'We'll be leaving soon, won't we?'

'We will,' he agreed curtly, and moved forward to meet the others, who by now had reached the beach in front of the palm-shaded house. Karen in fact had begun to run, and a moment later she was telling Amy pantingly, 'Oh, Amy, we have some bad news——'

'What?' Amy's face paled with shock. 'Is it—is it Aunt Evelyn?'

Karen shook her head. Mike had stepped aside with Paul, who was talking to him in a low voice.

'It's Clifford,' said Karen. 'He's been in a motor accident—the hospital in Cairns rang through this morning to tell us he was asking for you. They wanted to know if we could locate you and let you know. Oh, I'm terribly sorry—in the middle of your honeymoon, and when you're going to Italy in a couple of days' time——'

Amy's eyes flew to Mike, and she discovered he was looking at her darkly. So Paul had told him the news too.

'How serious is it?' she heard him ask the question sharply, and Karen said, 'I just don't know. He was—he was in the operating theatre. What will you do? Oh, isn't it terrible for poor Amy! How soon were you going?'

'To Italy?' Mike asked, frowning. 'Tomorrow evening, as a matter of fact. But Amy doesn't have to come —if necessary she can stay in Cairns.'

Karen stared at him. 'But Mike, you can't possibly go away without Amy! You can see Pauline and Sandro later—nothing's going to happen that can't wait. You'll have to put it off.'

'Look, Karen,' Mike said harshly, 'I'll arrange my own life. Don't try to tell me what I should or shouldn't do.' He turned to Paul. 'Thanks for bringing the message. Amy and I will talk it over. As it happens we're all packed up now. We were planning to leave in the next hour. I'd be grateful if you'd arrange to have a car at the jetty so that we can go straight out to the airstrip.'

'I'll do that,' said Paul, sounding businesslike and formal. 'There's nothing else we can do?'

'Not a thing. We'll let you know the situation from Cairns.'

'I hope Clifford's going to be all right,' said Karen, lingering though Paul had started back towards the jetty. 'Even though you broke your engagement to him, I know you're still very fond of him, Amy.'

'That's enough, Karen—on your way,' Mike rapped out, and his sister sent him a reproachful look.

'You sound so hard, Mike. Surely you can understand? Amy cares a lot about Clifford, it's only natural.'

Amy looked at her helplessly. She wished Karen would keep quiet, and after a second she turned and hurried into the house, and in the bedroom began to check over her luggage tremblingly. The full meaning of what had happened hadn't struck her yet, but now it all began to sink in. Clifford was badly hurt—asking for her. How different it would be if she and Mike were close! Of course she cared about Clifford, but Karen had made it sound as if her feelings for him were much stronger than they were. She hoped and hoped that he was going to live, and she realised that now Mike would have the perfect excuse for leaving her behind when he went to Italy. Yet if Clifford were really dangerously injured—surely Mike wouldn't leave her on her own then. Yet perhaps he would. He was a hard man, and he had made up his mind.

He came inside presently to collect his own things, and when he spoke to her it was with a kind of remote consideration.

'You'll be able to stay in my house in Cairns for as long as you need, Amy. I won't leave you till we're exactly sure of what's happening, so don't worry, and for your sake, I hope Clifford's going to be all right ... Are you ready now?'

She nodded. Her eyes had filled with tears, and she longed to throw herself into his arms and cry there. Instead, with a feeling of fatality, she allowed him to take charge of her luggage and a moment later, her head slightly bowed to hide her quivering mouth, she left the house with him. Never to return, she thought, despair in her heart ...

On the other side of the island, everything had been organised. A car took them to the air-strip and Mike's plane, and it seemed no time at all till they were over Cairns Airport. Amy was conscious of concern for her though he said little, but in actual fact she was thinking far less about Clifford than she was about losing Mike, and as they came down on the air-strip she said bitterly, 'I suppose this will suit you very well. Everyone will understand why you've left me behind, and they'll think I——' Her voice broke and she stopped. They'd think she'd—dropped him.

Mike gave her a quick hard look. 'I've told you, Amy, if Clifford's condition's critical, I won't leave you on your own.'

'And—and if he should die?' she couldn't stop herself from saying, and she saw his jaw tighten.

'We'll think of that only if we have to.'

Amy felt despair. Mike was through with her. She could hear it in his voice.

His car had been brought to the airport, and he drove her straight to town and to the hospital—a big modern building that towered over the bungalows around it. He didn't go in with her, merely telling her tersely, 'You can telephone me at the bungalow if you need to. I'll be there all day, and if there's anything I can do, don't hesitate to ask me.'

Their eyes met and Amy felt troubled. She bit her lip as Mike reached out unexpectedly and took her hand, holding it tightly for a moment. 'I'm sorry this has happened, Amy. It's the last thing I'd have wished for you.'

He drove off then, and she went alone into the hospital, choking back tears. She wished he would have come in with her, but of course as far as he was concerned, their relationship was finished. If Clifford should die, she would really present him with a problem. But if Clifford should be all right, then Mike would leave her—tomorrow—without a qualm.

Clifford's operation was over, but he hadn't come out of the anaesthetic, and the Sister in charge of the ward took Amy to a small sitting room where she could wait, and spoke to her reassuringly.

'He had a wonderful surgeon, and he's young— healthy. But I can't pretend that today's not critical. I'm so glad you were able to get here. We didn't know who to contact when he was brought in. He kept muttering 'Amy' and in a rather roundabout way we managed to discover who you were.'

'Who told you?' Amy asked.

'Well, we found out from the telephone exchange

that he lived alone, but they put us through to some neighbours—Italians—who suggested we should ring the Hotel Bangalo. You're a relative, are you, Mrs Saunders?'

Amy coloured. It gave her a shock to hear herself called that. 'No, I'm not a relative. But Clifford worked for my uncle and I've known him since I was fourteen. He—he doesn't have any close relatives.'

The Sister patted her arm. 'You mustn't worry too much. I'm sure everything will be all right.'

'I hope so,' Amy murmured.

She stayed at the hospital for the rest of the day, and though she was allowed into Clifford's room for a few minutes early in the afternoon, he wasn't sufficiently conscious to recognise her, and in fact he called her Margaret. He was under close supervision for some time, but late in the afternoon the ward Sister told her that the doctor was very satisfied with his condition. His injuries had been to his chest, and there had been some internal damage, but he was definitely out of danger.

Amy was allowed in to see him again, and by now he was fairly lucid, and he recognised her at once and spoke her name.

After a while she asked him, 'Clifford, would you like me to let Margaret Leslie know you're here?'

'She won't come,' he muttered. 'We had a row.'

'Over—me?'

'Yes,' he groaned. 'I treated you badly, Amy. I felt a cur.'

'Don't, Clifford.' She took his hand in hers comfortingly, and he asked,

'Are you happy, Amy? You didn't marry Mike Saunders just because you found out about me and Margaret?'

'No, of course not, Clifford.' She managed a laugh that was half a sob.

'I should have come to your wedding,' he said. 'I've made a mess of everything.'

Presently he slept, and Amy left the room. She had done some thinking since she had heard Clifford muttering Margaret's name, and she decided to call her and tell her about the accident. The row she and Clifford had had might not be final, and if Margaret really cared about him, then she would want to know—want to see him, to put things right. At any rate, it was up to her and Clifford.

She found a telephone, and got through to Margaret in her home. She didn't say Clifford had been asking for her or that she should go and see him, she simply told her that the accident had been bad, but that he was now out of danger.

'I thought you might want to know,' she concluded.

'Thank you,' said Margaret. 'I'll certainly go and see him.' She hung up and Amy made a slight face. As calm as that! But at least she cared enough to visit him.

It gave her a strange sense of freedom, yet it was a freedom that seemed of little use to her. She longed to ring Mike and tell him the news—have him come to the hospital and pick her up, take her back to his house, spoil her—— Well, he'd come and pick her up, but he wouldn't spoil her, and the full realisation came to her that now he would quite certainly be leaving Cairns tomorrow—going to Italy, leaving her for good—and she felt desperately unhappy.

She didn't ring Mike. She walked into town, found somewhere to have a cup of coffee and a sandwich, then she walked along the Esplanade under the trees in the darkness. She couldn't lose Mike—she couldn't bear it. She'd convince him she was over Clifford—she'd share

him with Delona—she'd do anything so long as he
didn't leave her. She'd promise him not to be a—a rag
doll, half a wife——

She began walking in the direction of the bungalow.
All these desperate plans—but she knew very well that
Mike could ignore all her outpourings and go his own
way. She knew too that love was important to her—and
if he didn't love her, then it would be best for them to
part. The simple, inescapable fact was, they should
never have married, and she didn't know why she had
ever thought it could work.

When she reached the house, there was a light in the
sitting room and the front door was open. She walked
in and he was there, and at the mere sight of him her
eyes filled with weak tears.

'Oh, Mike——!' He had got to his feet and Amy
blundered across the room and into his arms, putting
her head against his chest and sobbing.

'Tell me,' he said hoarsely against her hair, 'is it bad?
I won't leave you, Amy.'

She heard her own hysterical laugh as she sobbed
out, 'He's all right—Clifford's going to be all right——'
She broke off because she was crying again.

'It's relief,' Mike commented. 'Well, have your cry.'
He kept his arms around her, and they stood there for
several minutes until she moved away from him and
wiped her eyes.

Their glances met, and he said coolly, 'You'd better
get to bed, Amy. You've had a hard time today, but it's
all over now. Do you need something to help you
sleep?'

She shook her head, all the things she had meant to
say to him spinning round in her mind. She couldn't
say them—not while he looked at her with those unreadable eyes.

'I guess you'll want to be up early in the morning to get back to the hospital,' he remarked. 'I'll take you round before I leave for Brisbane—I'll be driving, so I want to leave early.'

Amy turned away from him hopelessly. 'Where shall I sleep?'

'In the bedroom you had before,' said Mike with a lift of his brows. Amy turned away, embarrassed. What else had she expected? He might have threatened once to give her a little more experience before they parted, but circumstances had changed since then.

He had put her luggage in her room, and had even taken out a pair of her pyjamas and laid them on the bed—the pyjamas he had said she wouldn't need to wear on her honeymoon. Her toilet things were out, her brush and comb were on the dressing table. Trying not to think, Amy got ready for bed, but all the time she was listening for him. She heard him go to his room, and after a long time she switched off her light, then stood beside the bed. After tomorrow morning she wouldn't see him again, and while reason told her it must be for the best she couldn't accept it. Moonlight came in at the window and she thought of the room they had shared on the island, and of the night—the one and only night—when Mike had made love to her. She had thought it the most beautiful initiation into married love that could ever have been—she had been certain they were going to be blissfully happy.

Now—tomorrow—Mike was leaving for Italy without her. They would have an early breakfast together and then Mike would take her to the hospital and leave her there. Perhaps he would kiss her goodbye, and perhaps he wouldn't. And it didn't really matter either way.

Barefoot, she crossed the room and stood in the

hallway. His doorway gaped blackly only feet away. She listened but could hear nothing. Had he gone to sleep, not caring what tomorrow was going to bring?

As though she couldn't help it, she moved towards his room.

'Mike——' Her voice was low, shaky.

'What's the matter, Amy?' Her eyes were used to the darkness, and she could see him sitting up in bed, his naked body dark against the whiteness of the sheets. 'Can't you sleep?'

'No, I can't.' Her voice was choked.

'I'll get you some brandy.'

'I don't want it.' Trembling, afraid, yet unable to help herself, Amy moved across to the bed and sat on the side of it, terrifyingly close to him—so close she could feel the warmth from his body. She wanted desperately to tell him that she loved him, but she couldn't manage it. She said, 'Mike, I've been thinking. I—I don't want a divorce. I don't see marriage that way—it's—serious. And it's too—too soon. Couldn't we try again?'

He reached for her and pulled her down on the bed beside him.

'Amy—Amy, did you have to come in here talking to me that way? I've told you I'll let you go. Do you think I can be happy with a marriage that's all a pretence? Do you imagine I'll be happy conscious that you're—*trying again*, for God's sake, when I make love to you? —knowing that you're wishing yourself in Clifford's arms? ... What's happened? Isn't he going to be able to——'

'He had chest injuries,' she interrupted. 'He'll be perfectly all right. But I don't want to go back to him, Mike. I don't want to. I couldn't—not ever. I—I love *you*.'

Her voice had grown almost inaudible, and the next minute she was crushed against him, and he was feverishly unbuttoning her pyjama top, while she wriggled free of it. She could feel his skin against hers, his hands warm on her naked body. His lips found her mouth and then, in spite of everything, she felt herself stiffen slightly.

Mike was aware of it at once.

'What's the matter?' he said against her lips, and she burst out despairingly,

'I know you only married me because you can't have Delona—because you want a wife and children.' There were tears on her cheeks and she could taste their saltiness as they ran down. 'I'm sorry—I'm sorry—I wasn't thinking of Clifford, I promise. Please—If you just——'

'If I just what?' Mike had thrust her away from him, and he sat up, and she knew he was looking down at her through the darkness. 'Amy,' he said, 'do you love me?'

'Yes,' she said despairingly. 'Oh yes! Since before we were married—more after—after that night when——'

'Then listen—will it surprise you all that much to know that I love you? That I pushed you into marrying me because I was afraid if I went to Italy without you, I'd have lost you? It's all as simple as that. So now will you shut up and come back to me?'

'But—Delona——' she began weakly. Mike had the rest of her pyjamas off now, and she had difficulty resisting him. 'What if Delona *did* get a divorce? Wouldn't you—want her then? Wouldn't you wish——'

He stopped her with his mouth against hers, and gradually her struggles ceased. It was only when she was completely unresisting that he desisted, and told her, 'Delona won't ever get a divorce. She's a one-man woman, and her husband's in a psychiatric hospital. She has complete faith that he'll recover.'

'But—she's your mistress,' she whispered, drowningly aware that all she wanted was for him to go on making love to her.

'Who told you that, for heaven's sake? She's not my mistress.'

'You stayed on Nerina that night——'

'And nothing happened that I didn't tell you about. Is that what's been bothering you? Listen, Amy, I love you. Get that firmly into your head, once and for all. As for Delona, I've never asked her to marry me, and never wanted to. We made love once, but it didn't work for either of us. Since then we've had a good relationship and a good understanding. Whereas with you—I wanted you the minute we met. Do you know I was so jealous of Clifford I could have killed him—before I knew any more about him other than that he was your fiancé.'

'You needn't be jealous,' she said, clinging to him. 'I forgot Clifford when I fell in love with you and began to discover what it was all about. Please—please don't leave me tomorrow!'

'As if I would!' Mike exulted. 'We'll go to Italy together—whenever you're ready. We'll see Florence—Venice——'

'Tomorrow,' she said, knowing that Clifford wouldn't need her, that Margaret would be there.

'Tomorrow,' he agreed, 'And by then, my darling,' he concluded, pulling her against him, 'we'll know a thousand more things about each other. We've the whole beautiful night ahead of us.' He touched her lips with his. 'Tell me again that you love me.'

'I love you,' she sighed, and his lips came down to claim hers.

What the press says about Harlequin romance fiction...

"When it comes to romantic novels...
Harlequin is the indisputable king."
>   —*New York Times*

"...exciting escapism, easy reading, interesting
characters and, always, a happy ending....
They are hard to put down."
>   — *Transcript-Telegram*, Holyoke (Mass.)

"...always...an upbeat, happy ending."
>   —*San Francisco Chronicle*

"...a work of art."
>   — *Globe & Mail*, Toronto

"Nothing quite like it has happened since
Gone With the Wind..."
>   —*Los Angeles Times*

Harlequin Presents...

Romance novels that speak
the language of love known to
women the world over.

Harlequin Presents...

A distinctive series of dramatic
love stories created
especially for you
by world-acclaimed
authors.

FREE!

A hardcover Romance Treasury volume
containing 3 treasured works of romance
by 3 outstanding Harlequin authors...

...as your introduction to Harlequin's
Romance Treasury subscription plan!

Romance Treasury

...almost 600 pages of exciting romance reading
every month at the low cost of $5.97 a volume!

A wonderful way to collect many of Harlequin's most beautiful love
stories, all originally published in the late '60s and early '70s.
Each value-packed volume, bound in a distinctive gold-embossed
leatherette case and wrapped in a colorfully illustrated dust jacket,
contains...
- 3 full-length novels by 3 world-famous authors of romance fiction
- a unique illustration for every novel
- the elegant touch of a delicate bound-in ribbon bookmark...
  and much, much more!

Romance Treasury

...for a library of romance you'll treasure forever!

Complete and mail today the FREE gift certificate and subscription
reservation on the following page.

Romance Treasury

An exciting opportunity to collect treasured works of romance! Almost 600 pages of exciting romance reading in each beautifully bound hardcover volume!

You may cancel your subscription whenever you wish! You don't have to buy any minimum number of volumes. Whenever you decide to stop your subscription just drop us a line and we'll cancel all further shipments.